jGN EVANS Dustin
Dinosaur drama /
ans Dustin

WITHDRAWN
APR 0 4 2013

D0597357

THE MYSTICAL PENCIL

DINOSAUR DRAMA

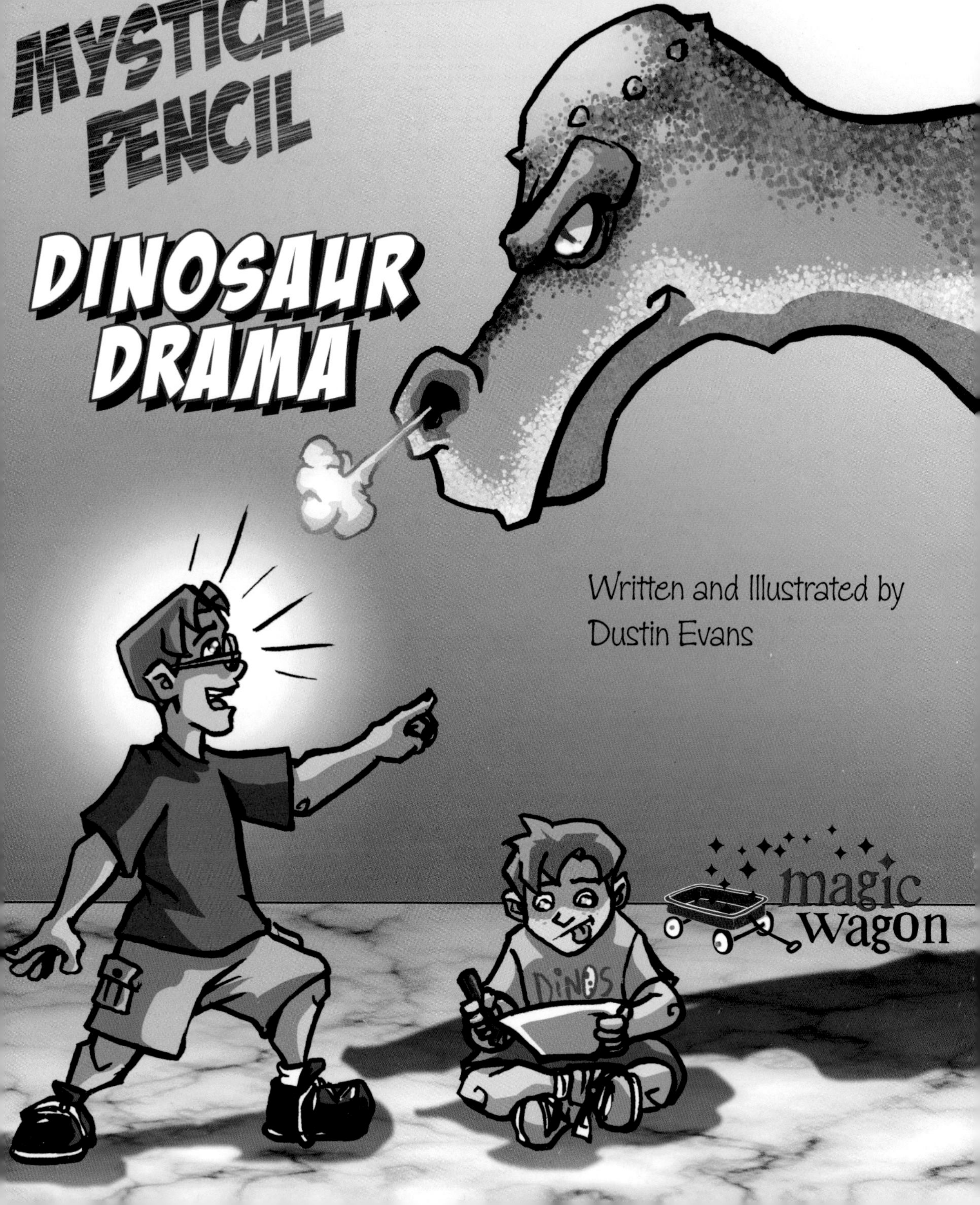
DINOS

Written and Illustrated by
Dustin Evans

magic wagon

visit us at
www.abdopublishing.com

Published by Magic Wagon, a division of the ABDO Group, PO Box 398166, Minneapolis, MN 55439. Copyright © 2013 by Abdo Consulting Group, Inc. International copyrights reserved in all countries. All rights reserved. No part of this book may be reproduced in any form without written permission from the publisher.

Graphic Planet™ is a trademark and logo of Magic Wagon.

Printed in the United States of America, North Mankato, Minnesota.
102012
012013
♲ This book contains at least 10% recycled materials.

Written and Illustrated by Dustin Evans
Edited by Stephanie Hedlund and Rochelle Baltzer
Cover art by Dustin Evans
Cover design by Neil Klinepier

Library of Congress Cataloging-in-Publication Data

Evans, Dustin, 1982-
  Dinosaur drama / written & illustrated by Dustin Evans.
    p. cm. -- (The mystical pencil)
  Summary: Alex decides that the only safe place for the mystical pencil is the museum where his father works--but when Marvin borrows the pencil and begins to draw dinosaurs, things quickly get out of hand.
  ISBN 978-1-61641-927-1
  1. Pencils--Comic books, strips, etc. 2. Pencils--Juvenile fiction. 3. Dinosaurs--Comic books, strips, etc. 4. Dinosaurs--Juvenile fiction. 5. Imagination--Comic books, strips, etc. 6. Imagination--Juvenile fiction. 7. Museums--Comic books, strips, etc. 8. Museums--Juvenile fiction. 9. Graphic novels. [1. Graphic novels. 2. Pencils--Fiction. 3. Dinosaurs--Fiction. 4. Imagination--Fiction. 5. Museums--Fiction. 6. Pencils--Fiction. 7. Imagination--Fiction.] I. Title.
  PZ7.7.E92Din 2013
  741.5'973--dc23
                    2012027939

Contents

Previously in *Raging Robots . . .*

Alex's dad returned from an archaeological dig and brought back many artifacts. When Alex needed a pencil to finish a project, he got an old, beat-up one from his dad's bag.

That beat-up pencil didn't look like much, but it had great powers. The monster Alex drew suddenly came to life! Alex had to think quickly to make things right. Soon, everything was back to normal... but one thing was missing —the Mystical Pencil!

Sara had found the pencil on the street and brought it to school. Alex and Sara worked together to keep the farm creatures she drew from turning the school into a pigpen!

Stewart later found the pencil and used it to draw robots for his science fair project. Alex, Sara, and Stewart managed to draw their way out of it. Now, Alex is trying to return the Mystical Pencil to his father at the museum. But the pencil is waiting for another adventure...

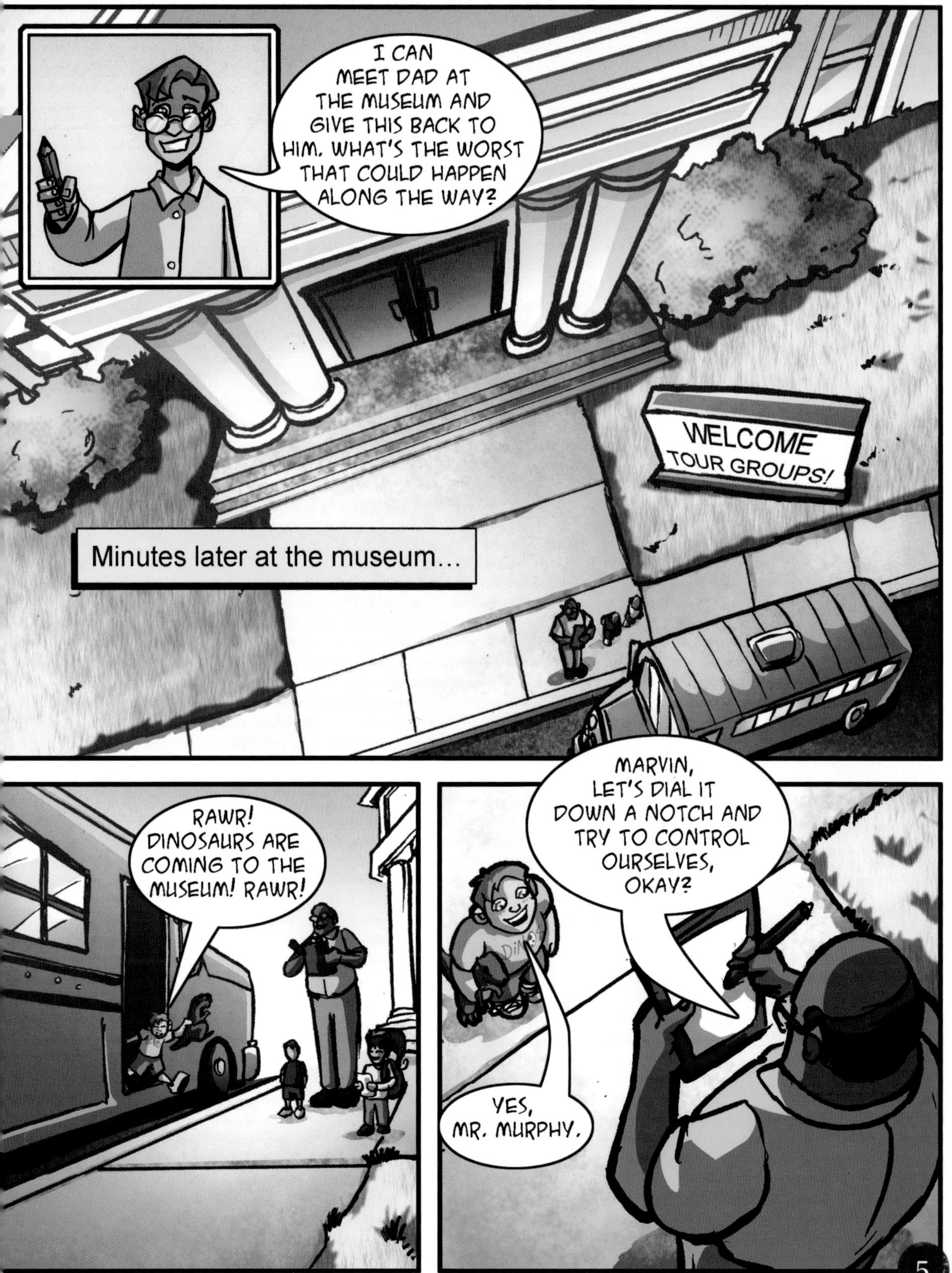
I CAN MEET DAD AT THE MUSEUM AND GIVE THIS BACK TO HIM. WHAT'S THE WORST THAT COULD HAPPEN ALONG THE WAY?
WELCOME TOUR GROUPS!
Minutes later at the museum…
RAWR! DINOSAURS ARE COMING TO THE MUSEUM! RAWR!
MARVIN, LET'S DIAL IT DOWN A NOTCH AND TRY TO CONTROL OURSELVES, OKAY?
YES, MR. MURPHY.

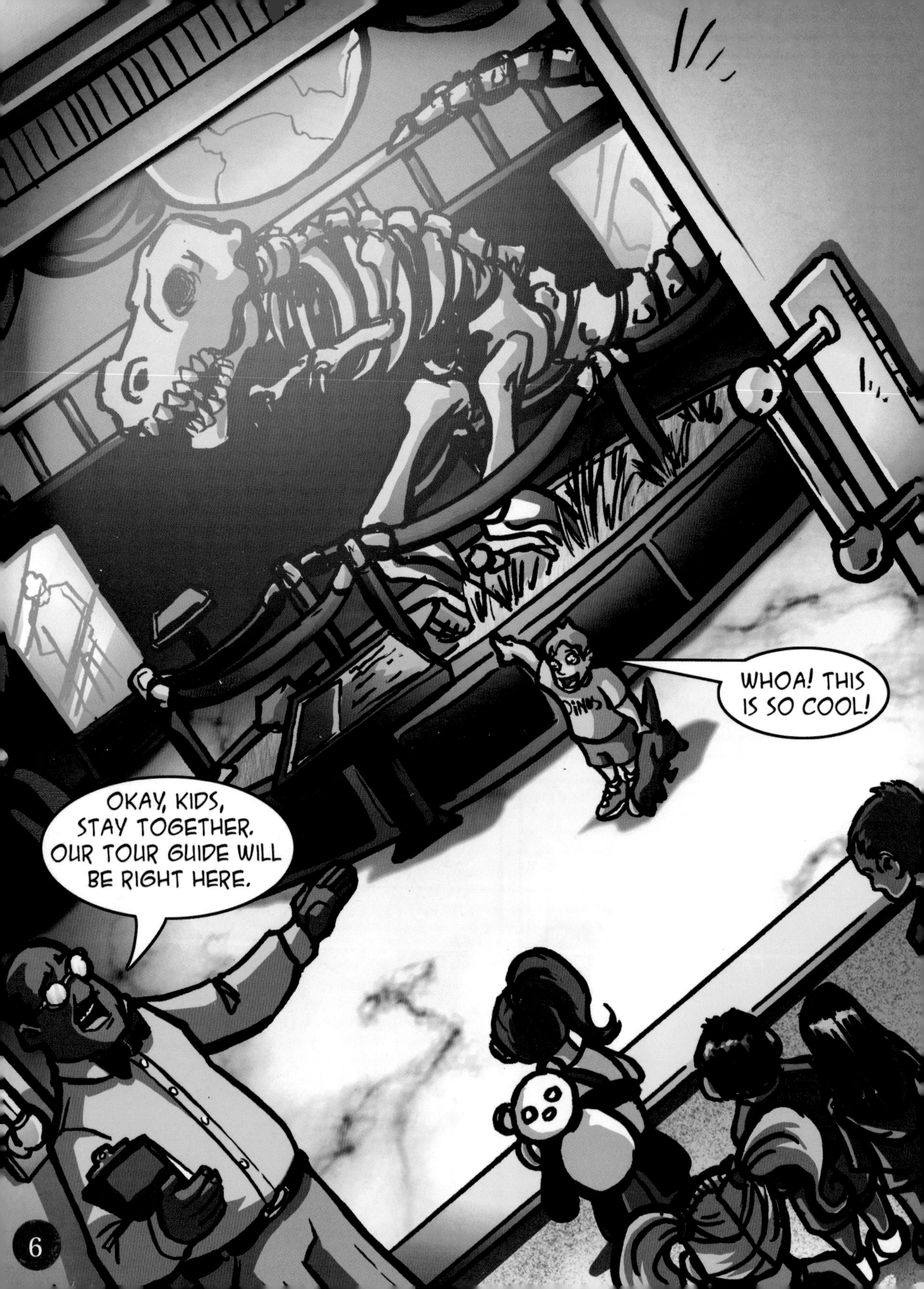
WHOA! THIS IS SO COOL!
OKAY, KIDS, STAY TOGETHER. OUR TOUR GUIDE WILL BE RIGHT HERE.

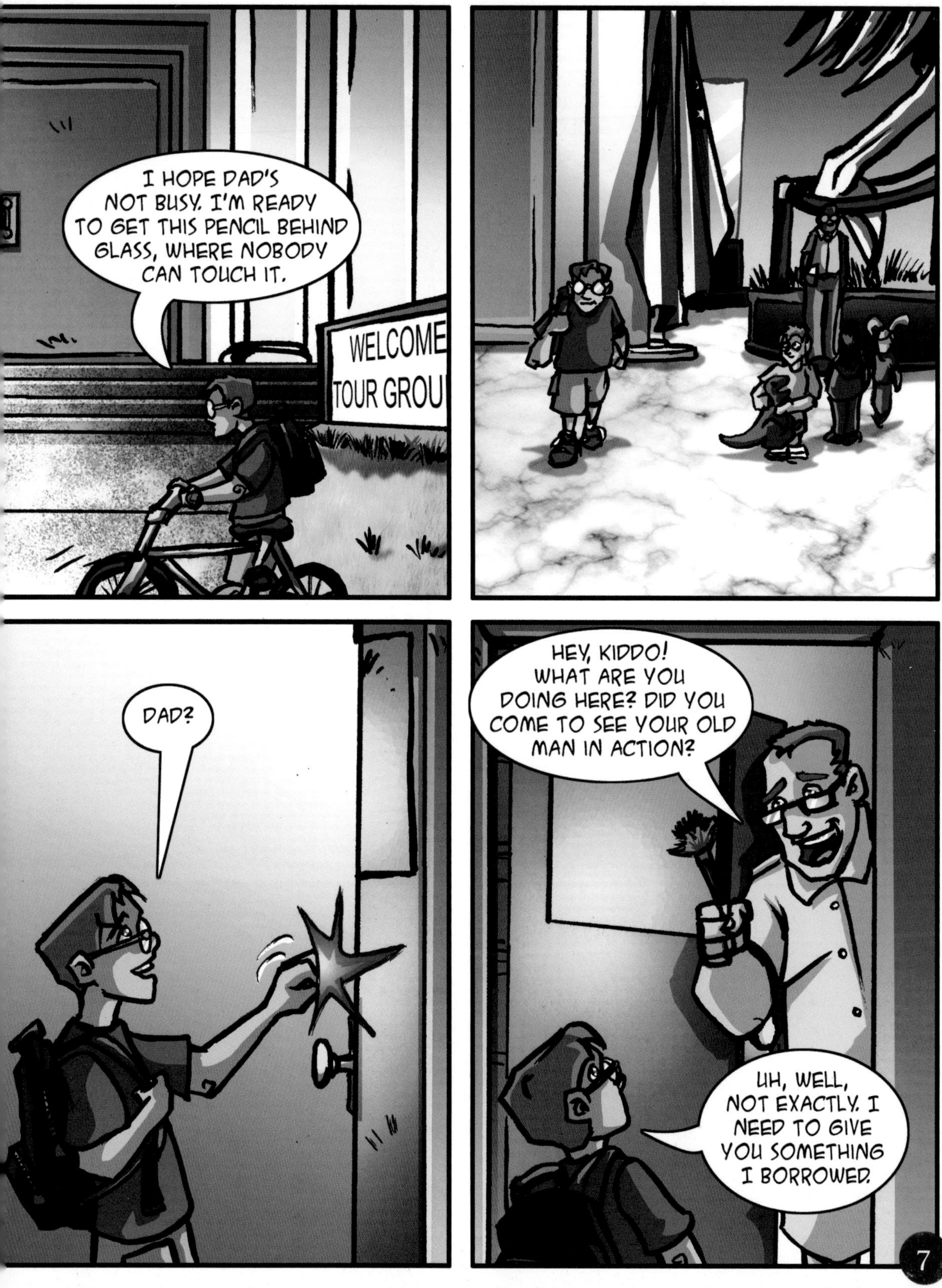
I HOPE DAD'S NOT BUSY. I'M READY TO GET THIS PENCIL BEHIND GLASS, WHERE NOBODY CAN TOUCH IT.
WELCOME
TOUR GROU
DAD?
HEY, KIDDO! WHAT ARE YOU DOING HERE? DID YOU COME TO SEE YOUR OLD MAN IN ACTION?
UH, WELL, NOT EXACTLY. I NEED TO GIVE YOU SOMETHING I BORROWED.

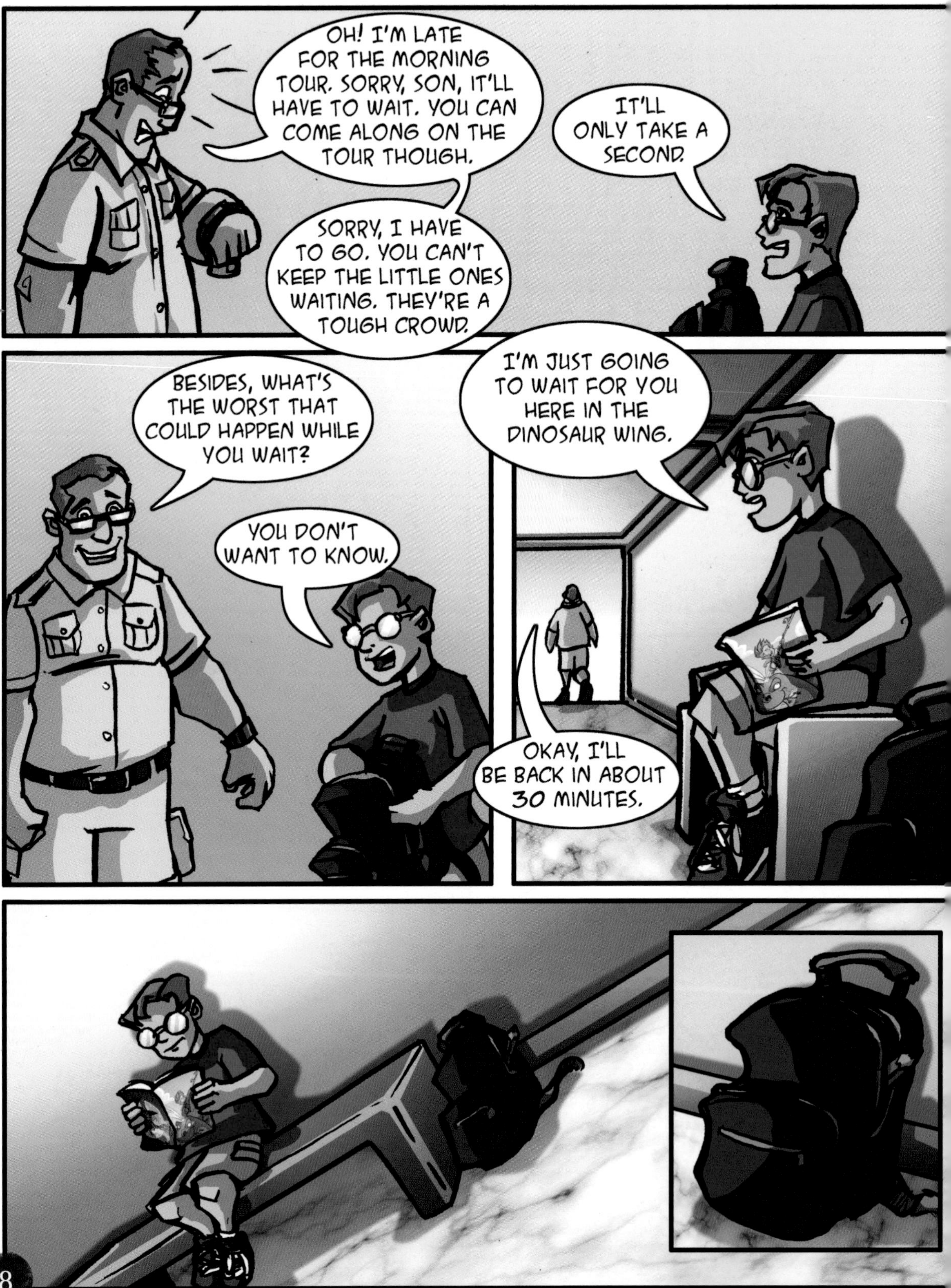
OH! I'M LATE FOR THE MORNING TOUR. SORRY, SON, IT'LL HAVE TO WAIT. YOU CAN COME ALONG ON THE TOUR THOUGH.
IT'LL ONLY TAKE A SECOND.
SORRY, I HAVE TO GO. YOU CAN'T KEEP THE LITTLE ONES WAITING. THEY'RE A TOUGH CROWD.
BESIDES, WHAT'S THE WORST THAT COULD HAPPEN WHILE YOU WAIT?
YOU DON'T WANT TO KNOW.
I'M JUST GOING TO WAIT FOR YOU HERE IN THE DINOSAUR WING.
OKAY, I'LL BE BACK IN ABOUT 30 MINUTES.

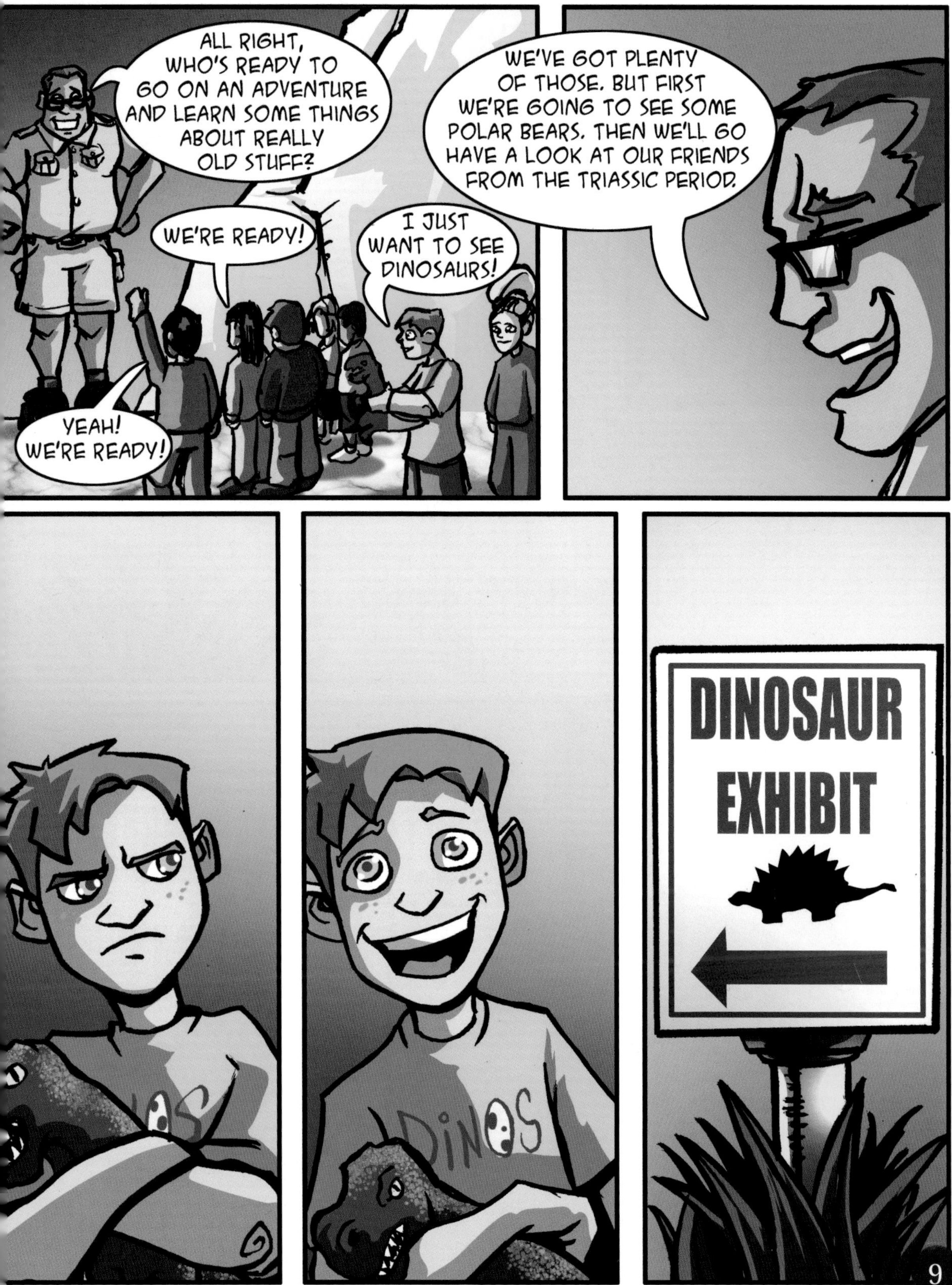
ALL RIGHT, WHO'S READY TO GO ON AN ADVENTURE AND LEARN SOME THINGS ABOUT REALLY OLD STUFF?
WE'RE READY!
I JUST WANT TO SEE DINOSAURS!
YEAH! WE'RE READY!
WE'VE GOT PLENTY OF THOSE. BUT FIRST WE'RE GOING TO SEE SOME POLAR BEARS. THEN WE'LL GO HAVE A LOOK AT OUR FRIENDS FROM THE TRIASSIC PERIOD.
DINOS
DINOSAUR EXHIBIT

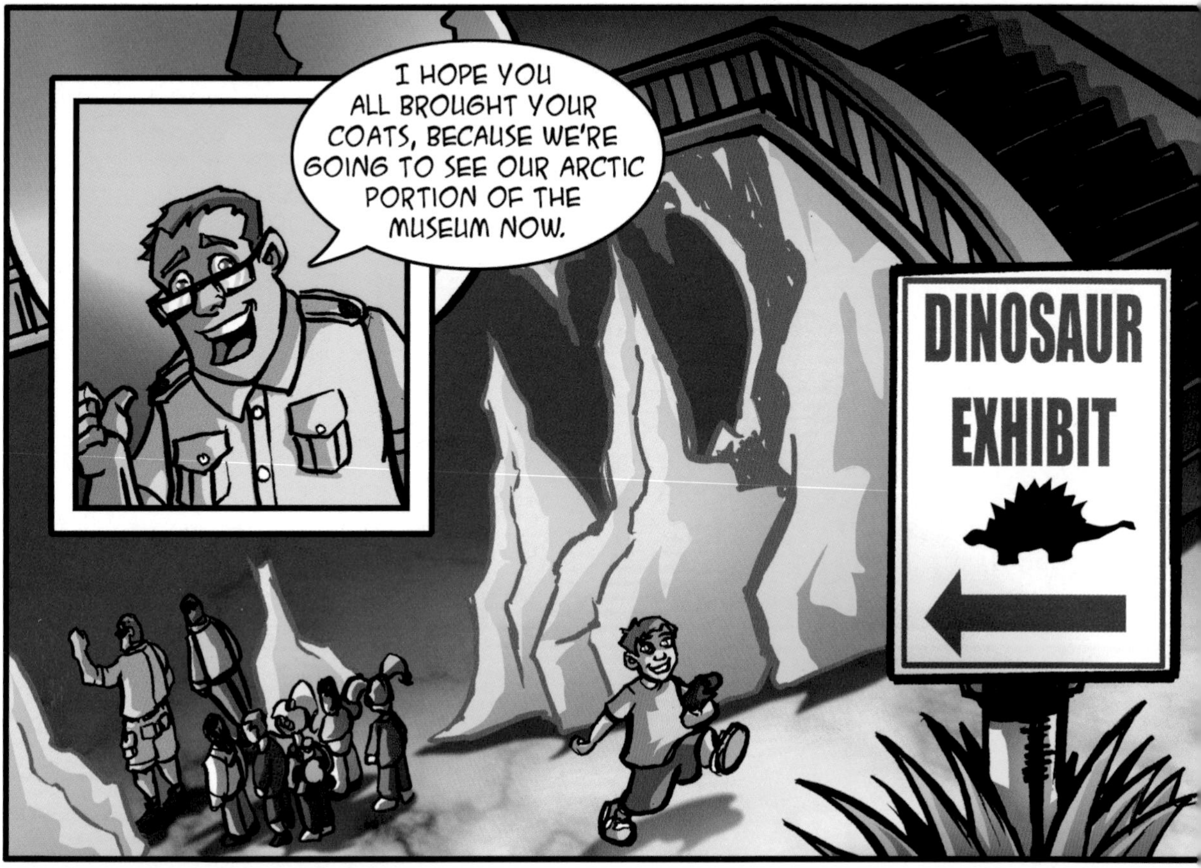
I HOPE YOU ALL BROUGHT YOUR COATS, BECAUSE WE'RE GOING TO SEE OUR ARCTIC PORTION OF THE MUSEUM NOW.
DINOSAUR EXHIBIT

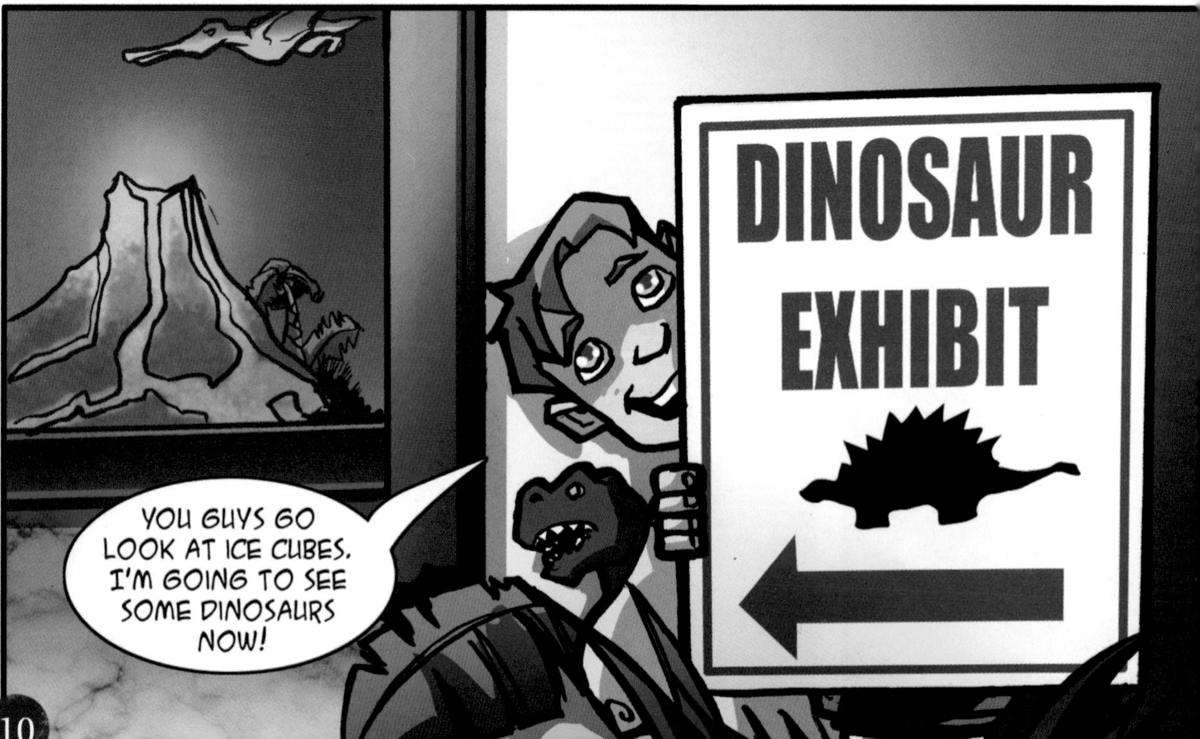
DINOSAUR EXHIBIT
YOU GUYS GO LOOK AT ICE CUBES. I'M GOING TO SEE SOME DINOSAURS NOW!

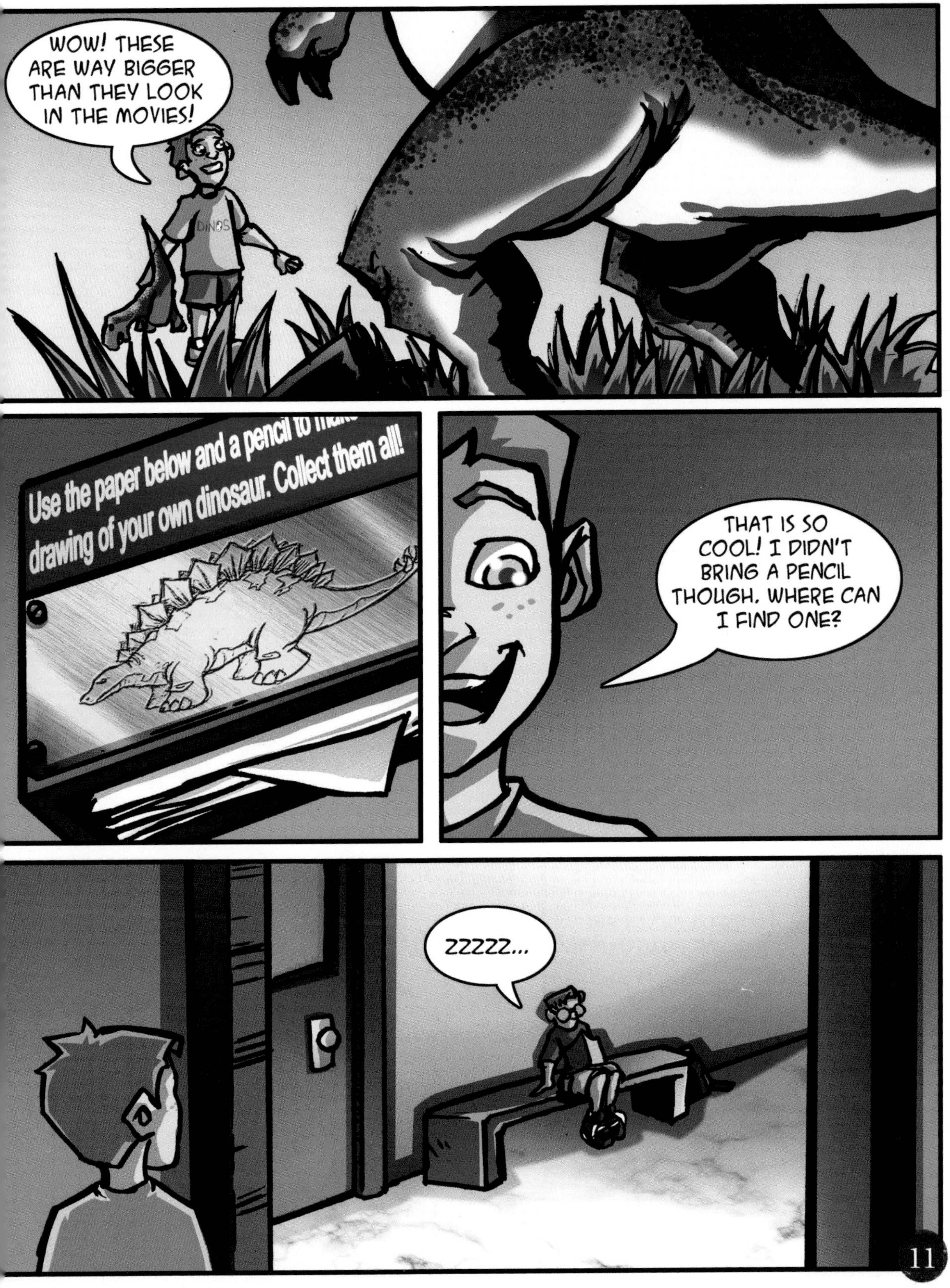
WOW! THESE ARE WAY BIGGER THAN THEY LOOK IN THE MOVIES!
DINOS
Use the paper below and a pencil to
drawing of your own dinosaur. Collect them all!
THAT IS SO COOL! I DIDN'T BRING A PENCIL THOUGH. WHERE CAN I FIND ONE?
ZZZZZ...

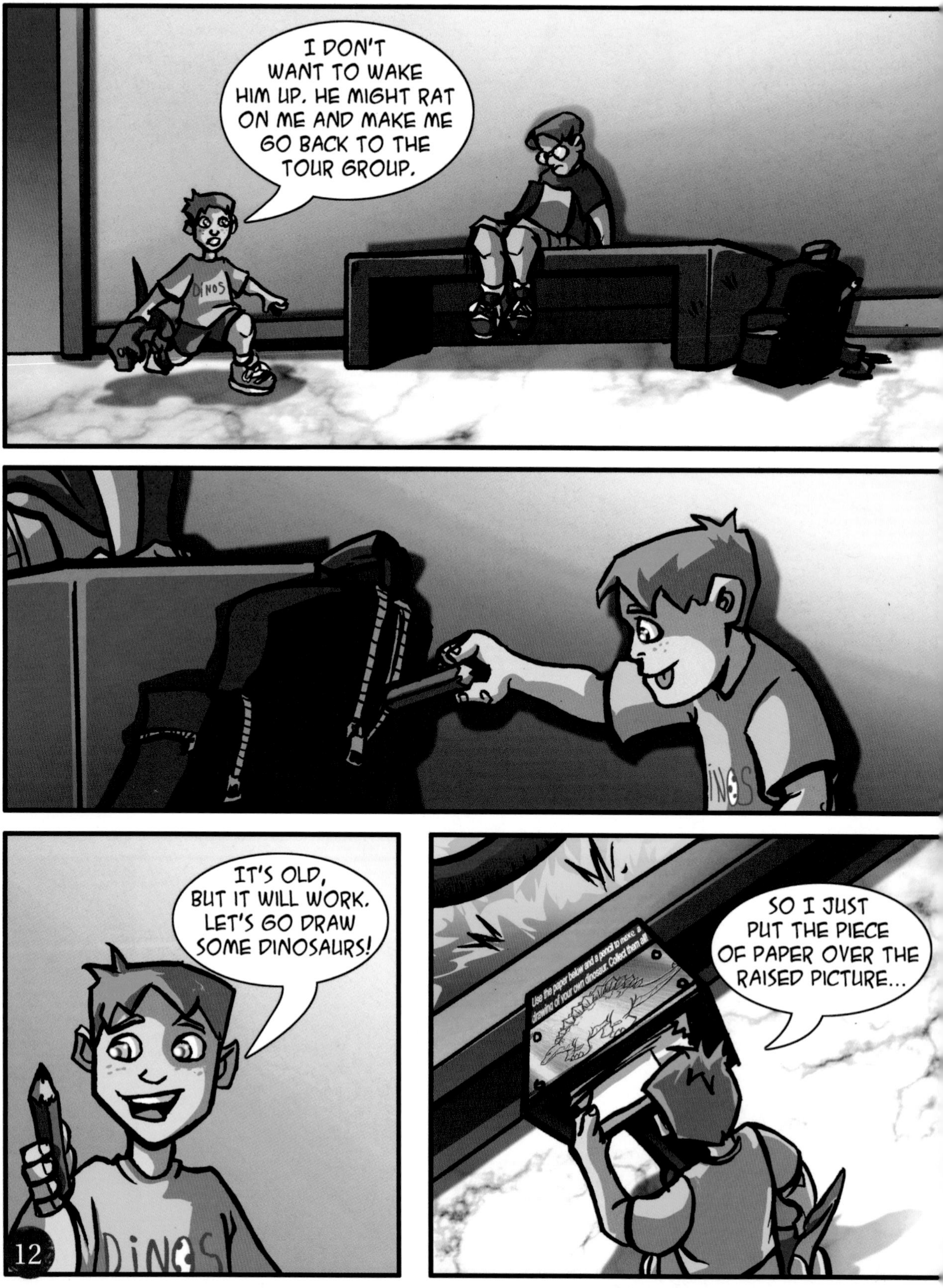
I DON'T WANT TO WAKE HIM UP. HE MIGHT RAT ON ME AND MAKE ME GO BACK TO THE TOUR GROUP.
DINOS
IT'S OLD, BUT IT WILL WORK. LET'S GO DRAW SOME DINOSAURS!
Use the paper below and a pencil to make a drawing of your own dinosaur. Collect them all!
SO I JUST PUT THE PIECE OF PAPER OVER THE RAISED PICTURE...

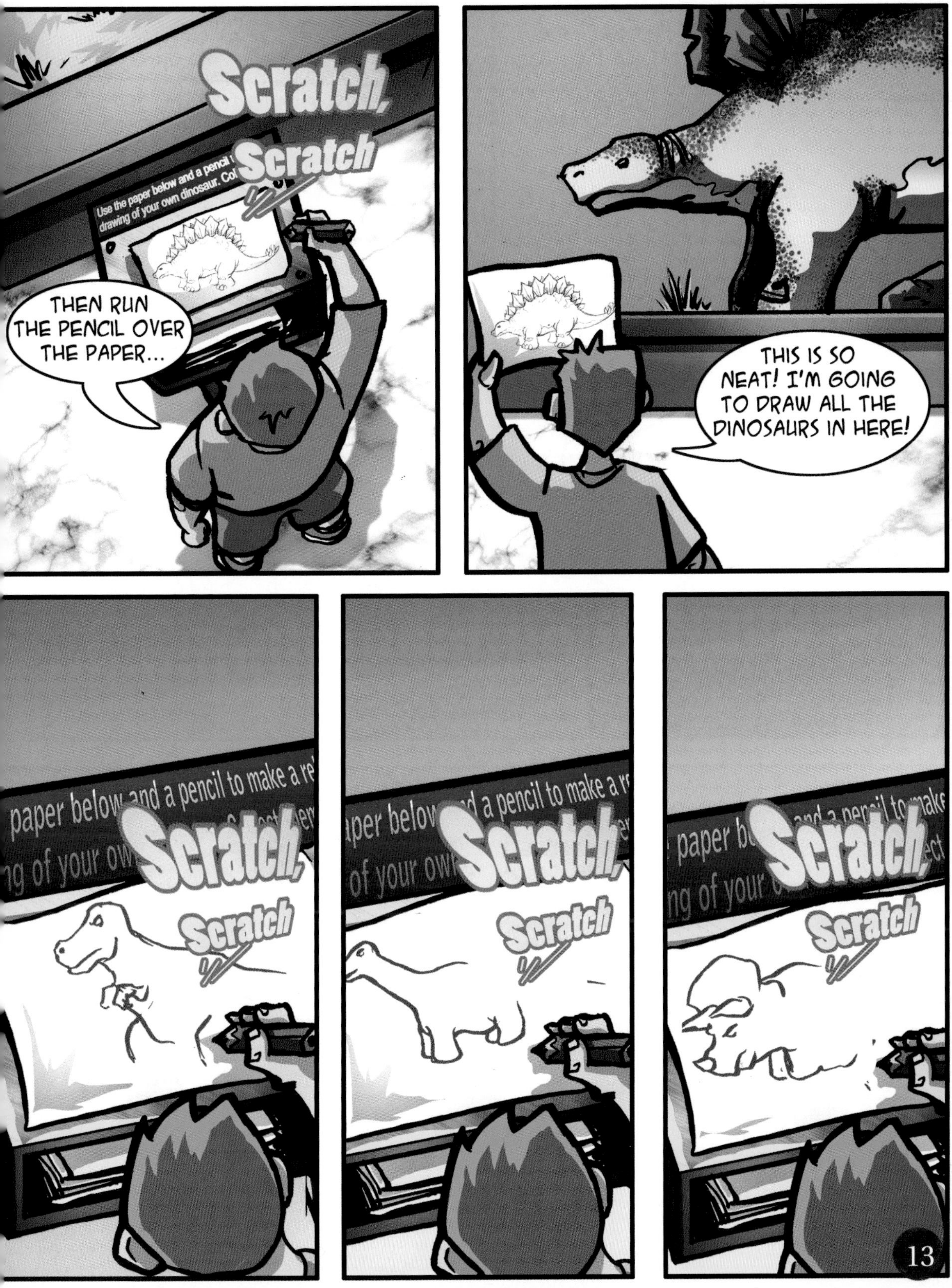
Scratch,
Scratch
THEN RUN THE PENCIL OVER THE PAPER...
THIS IS SO NEAT! I'M GOING TO DRAW ALL THE DINOSAURS IN HERE!
Scratch,
Scratch
Scratch,
Scratch
Scratch,
Scratch

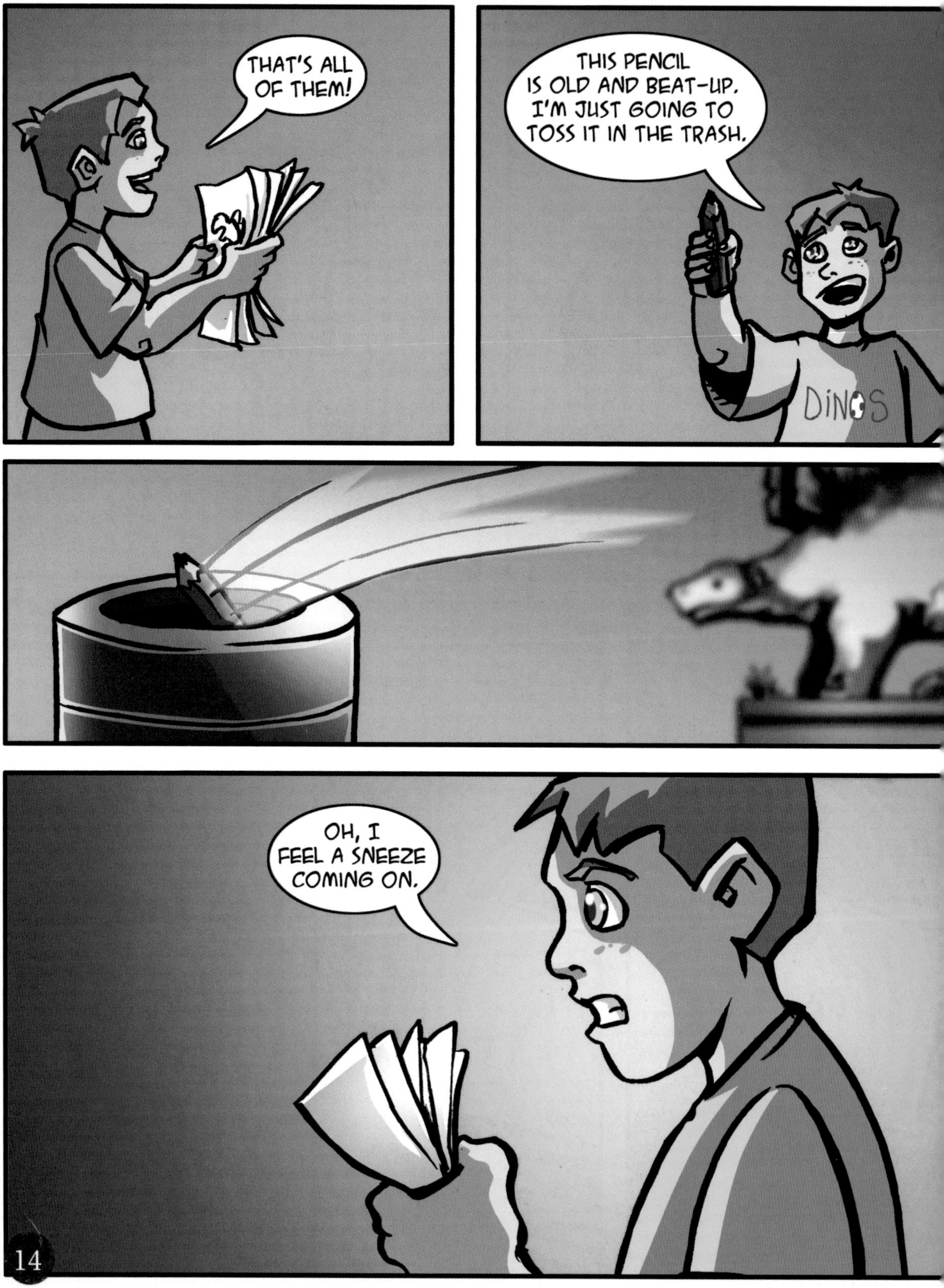
THAT'S ALL OF THEM!
THIS PENCIL IS OLD AND BEAT-UP. I'M JUST GOING TO TOSS IT IN THE TRASH.
DINOS
OH, I FEEL A SNEEZE COMING ON.

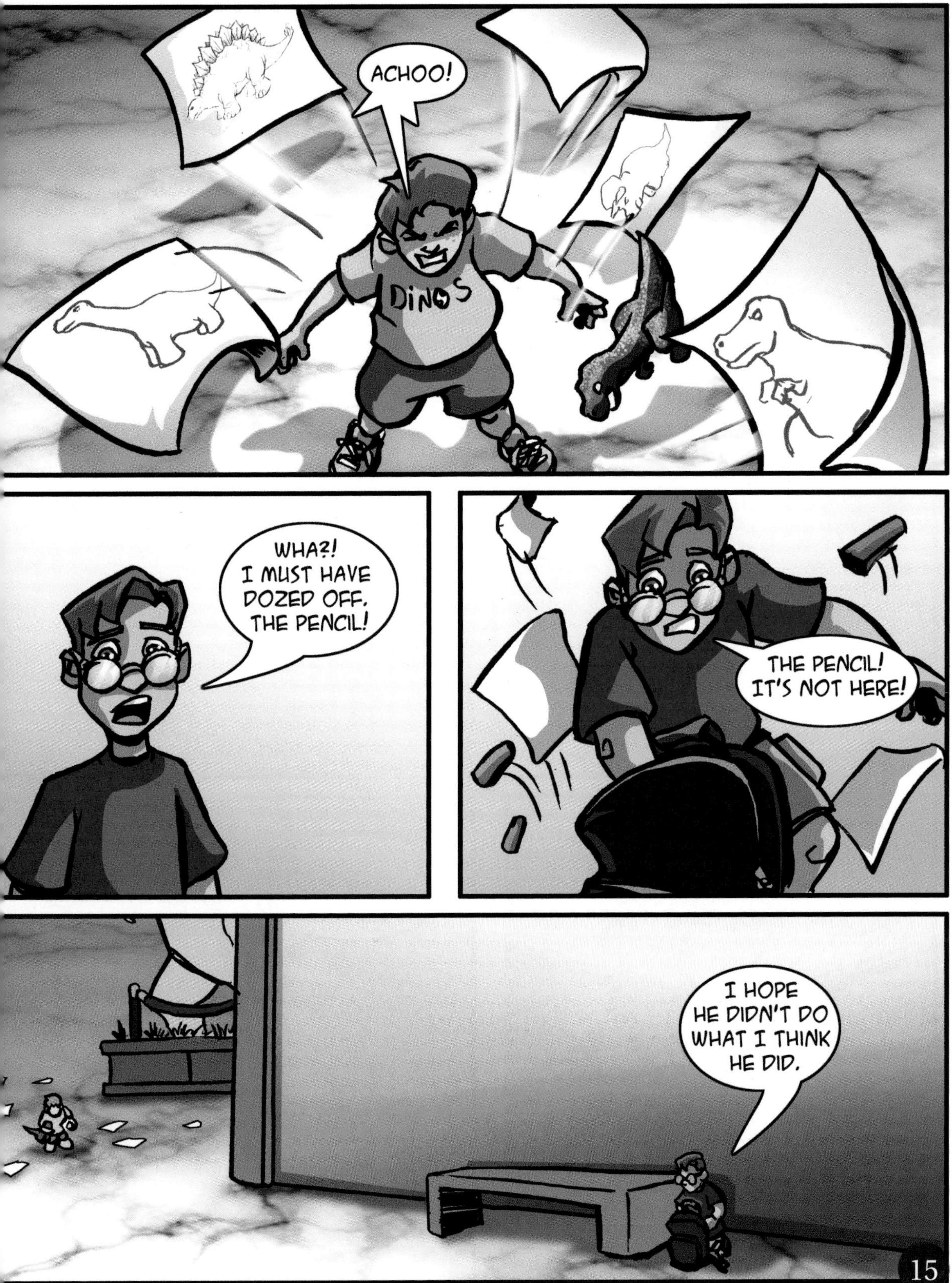
ACHOO!
DINOS
WHA?! I MUST HAVE DOZED OFF. THE PENCIL!
THE PENCIL! IT'S NOT HERE!
I HOPE HE DIDN'T DO WHAT I THINK HE DID.

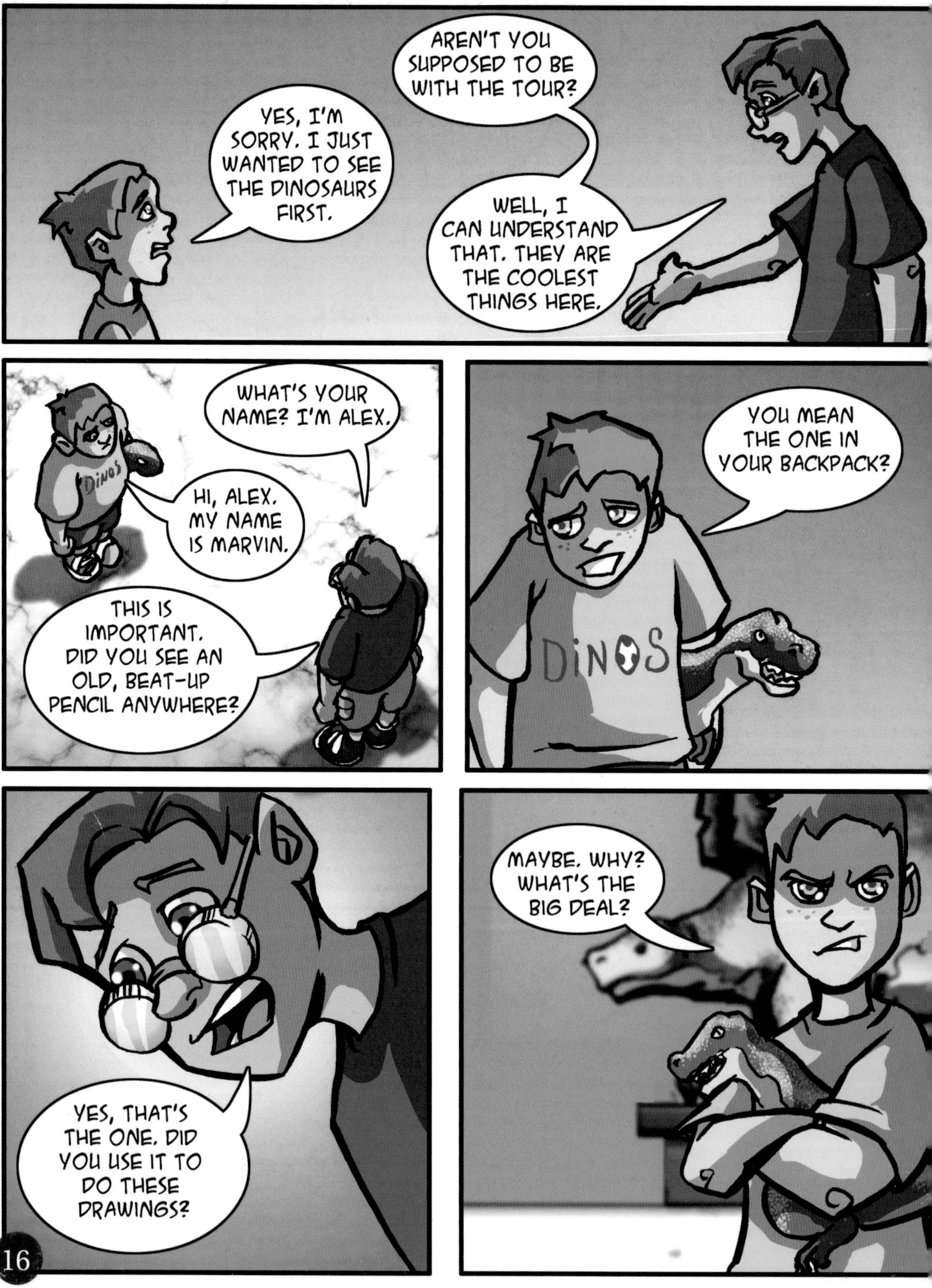
AREN'T YOU SUPPOSED TO BE WITH THE TOUR?
YES, I'M SORRY. I JUST WANTED TO SEE THE DINOSAURS FIRST.
WELL, I CAN UNDERSTAND THAT. THEY ARE THE COOLEST THINGS HERE.
DINOS
WHAT'S YOUR NAME? I'M ALEX.
HI, ALEX. MY NAME IS MARVIN.
THIS IS IMPORTANT. DID YOU SEE AN OLD, BEAT-UP PENCIL ANYWHERE?
YOU MEAN THE ONE IN YOUR BACKPACK?
DINOS
YES, THAT'S THE ONE. DID YOU USE IT TO DO THESE DRAWINGS?
MAYBE. WHY? WHAT'S THE BIG DEAL?

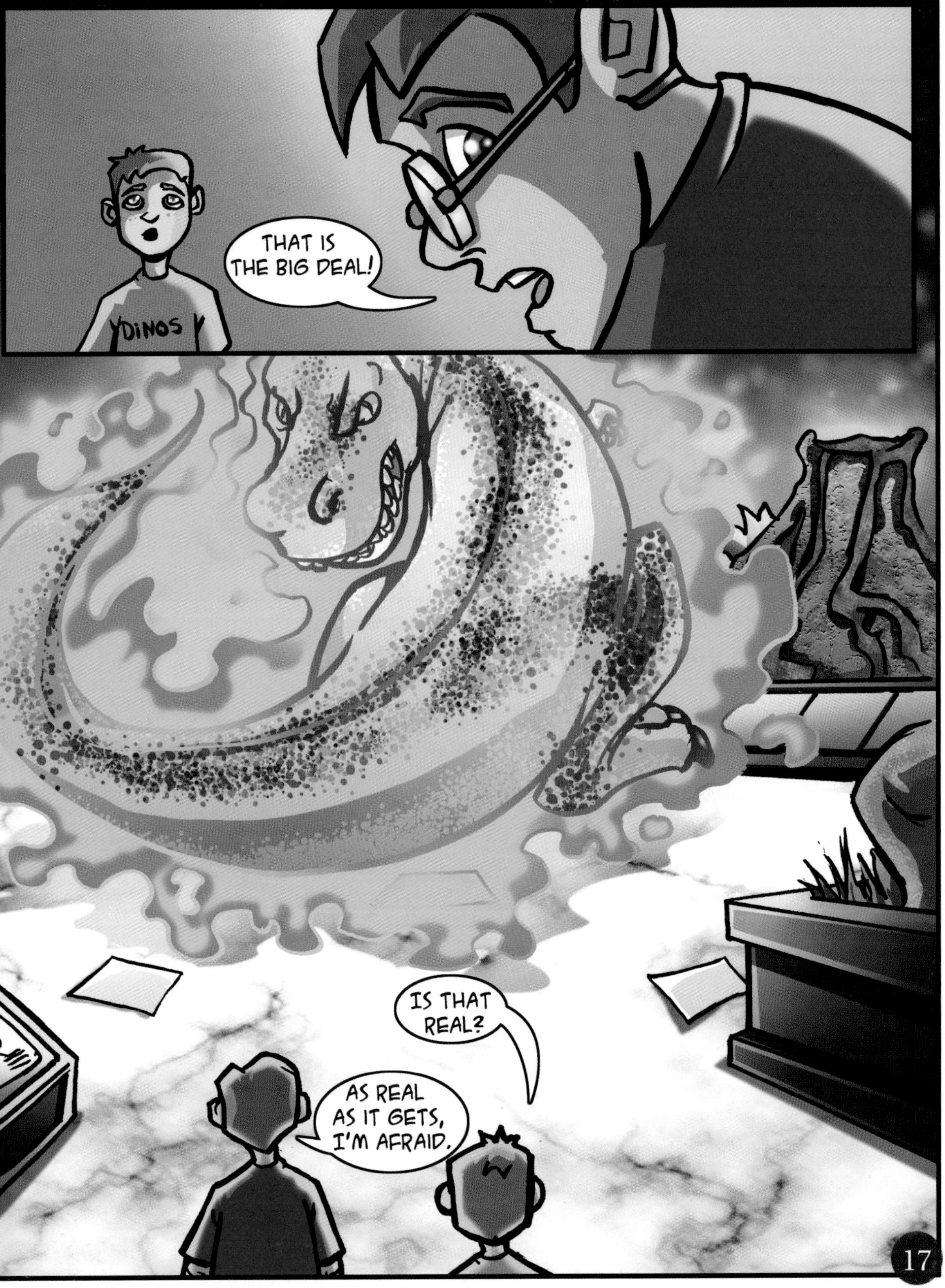
THAT IS THE BIG DEAL!
DINOS
IS THAT REAL?
AS REAL AS IT GETS, I'M AFRAID.

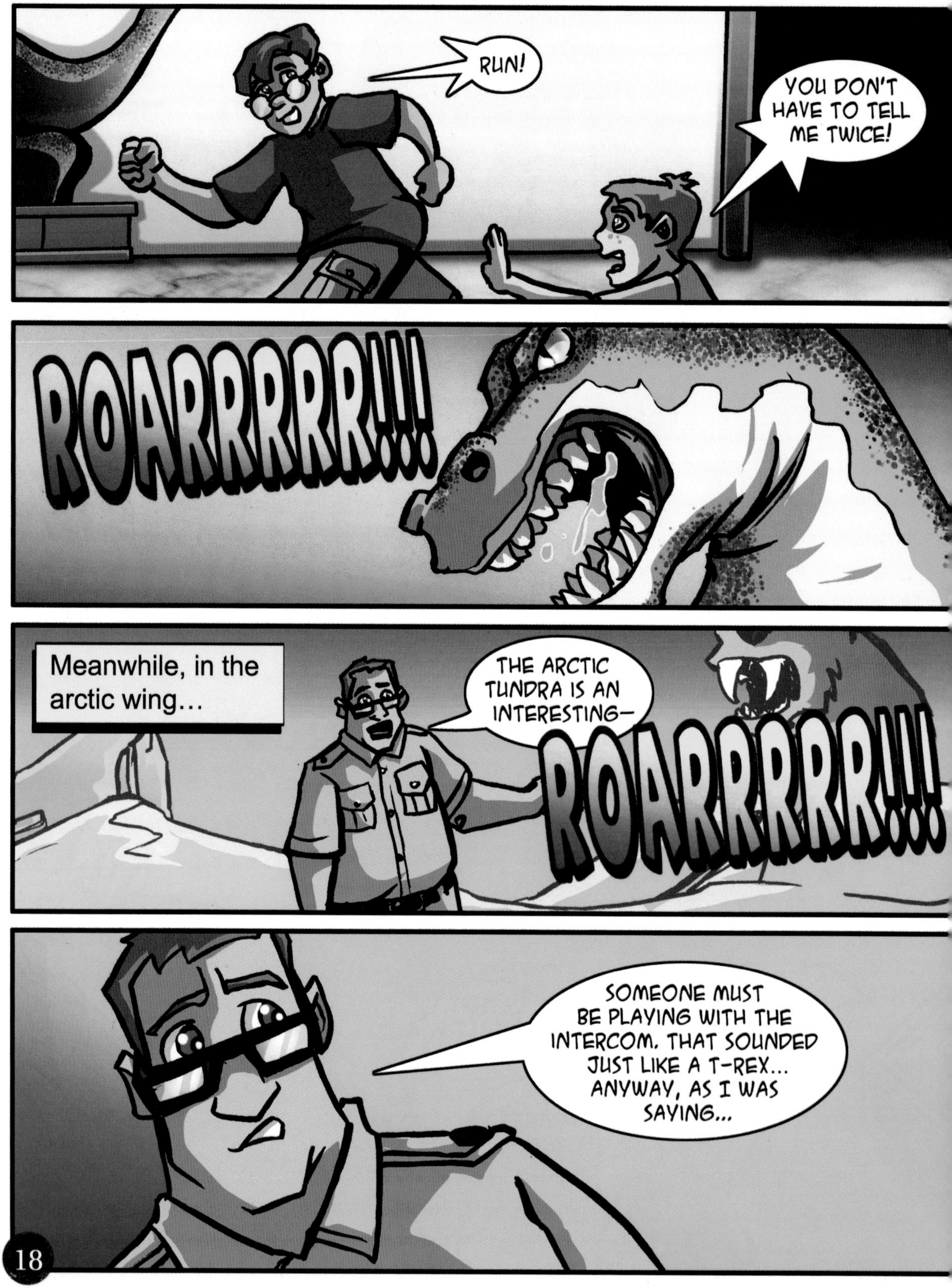
RUN!
YOU DON'T HAVE TO TELL ME TWICE!
ROARRRRR!!!
Meanwhile, in the arctic wing…
THE ARCTIC TUNDRA IS AN INTERESTING—
ROARRRRR!!!
SOMEONE MUST BE PLAYING WITH THE INTERCOM. THAT SOUNDED JUST LIKE A T-REX… ANYWAY, AS I WAS SAYING…

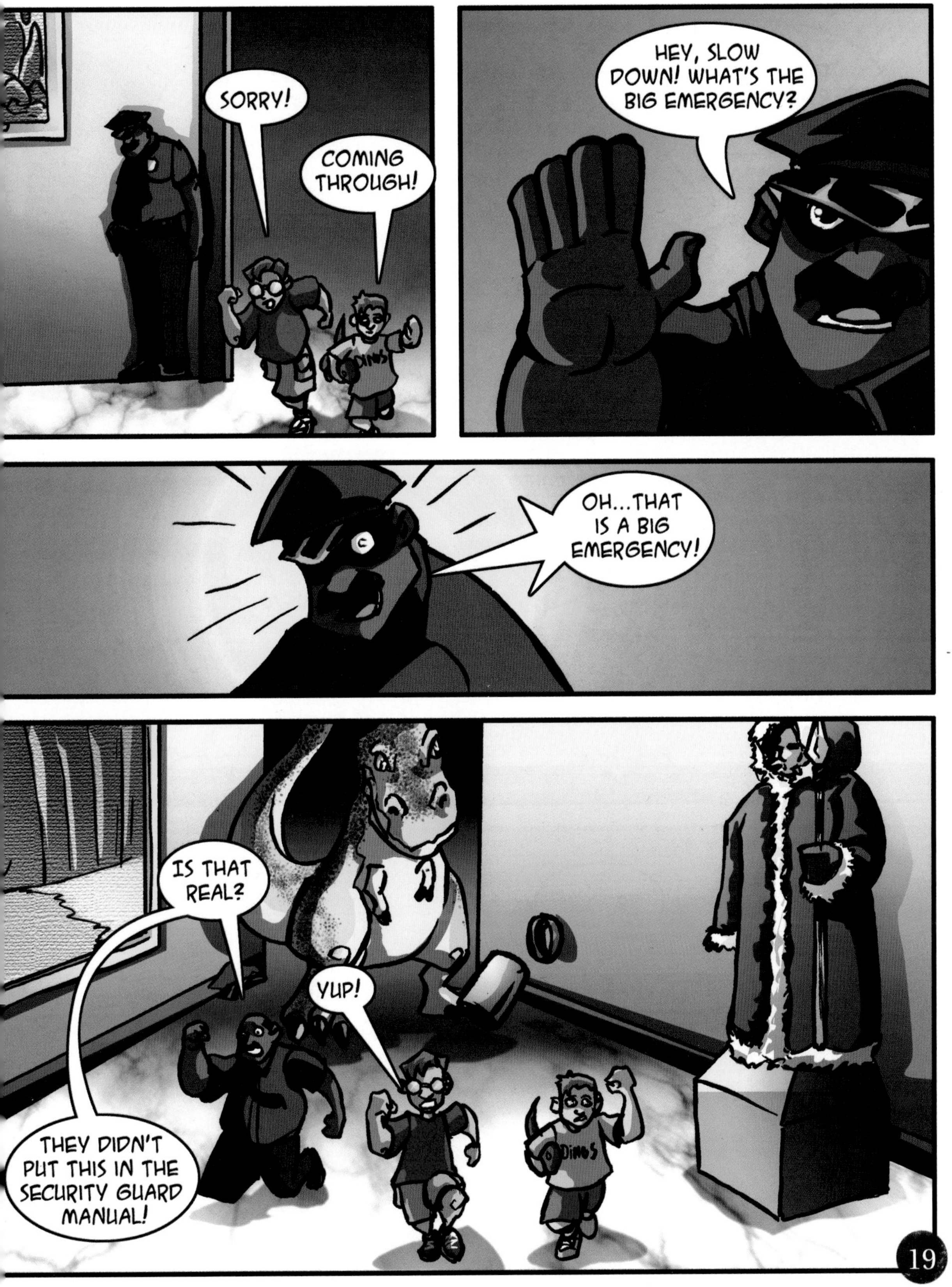

SORRY!
COMING THROUGH!
HEY, SLOW DOWN! WHAT'S THE BIG EMERGENCY?
OH...THAT IS A BIG EMERGENCY!
IS THAT REAL?
YUP!
THEY DIDN'T PUT THIS IN THE SECURITY GUARD MANUAL!

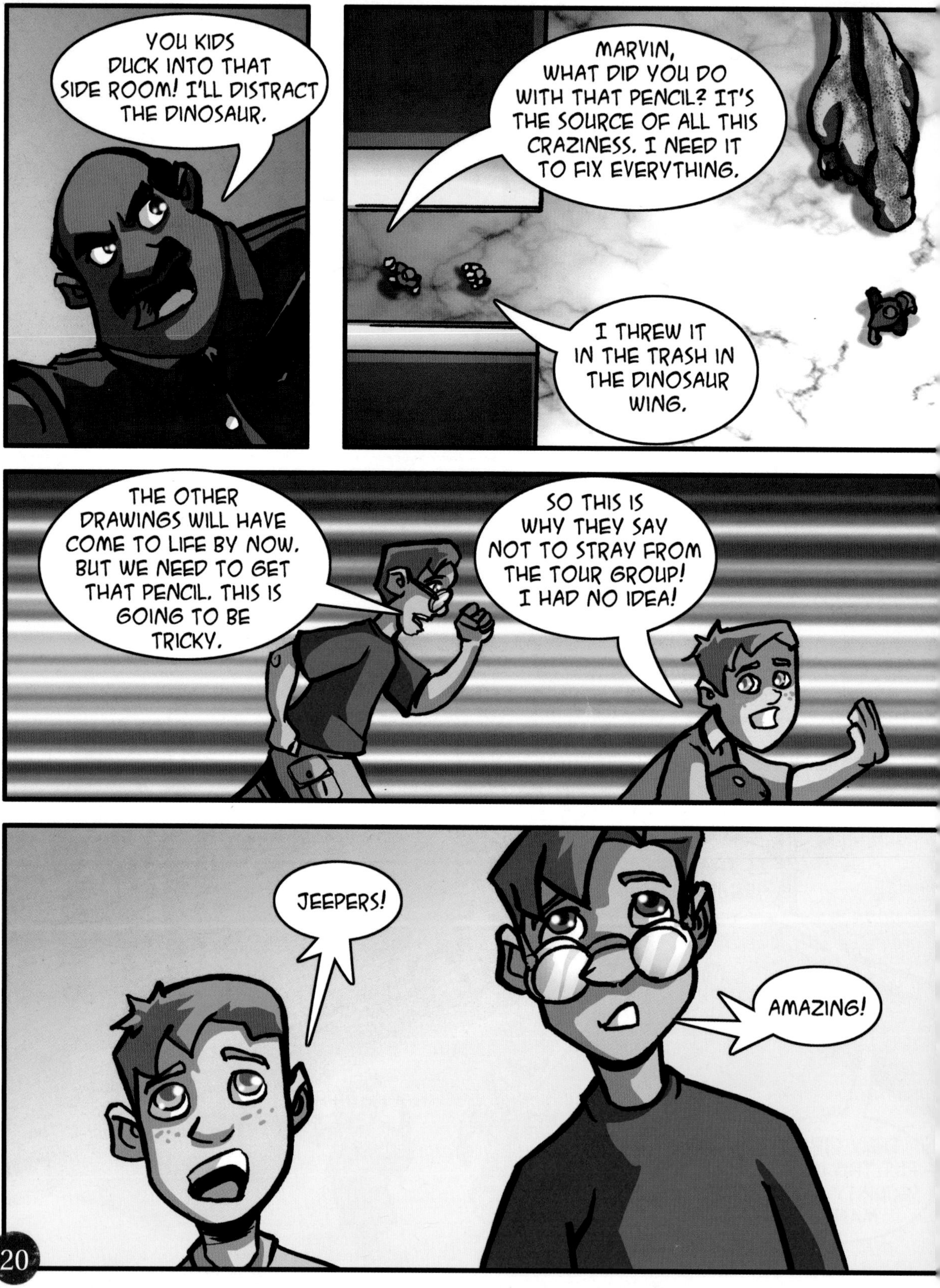
YOU KIDS DUCK INTO THAT SIDE ROOM! I'LL DISTRACT THE DINOSAUR.
MARVIN, WHAT DID YOU DO WITH THAT PENCIL? IT'S THE SOURCE OF ALL THIS CRAZINESS. I NEED IT TO FIX EVERYTHING.
I THREW IT IN THE TRASH IN THE DINOSAUR WING.
THE OTHER DRAWINGS WILL HAVE COME TO LIFE BY NOW. BUT WE NEED TO GET THAT PENCIL. THIS IS GOING TO BE TRICKY.
SO THIS IS WHY THEY SAY NOT TO STRAY FROM THE TOUR GROUP! I HAD NO IDEA!
JEEPERS!
AMAZING!

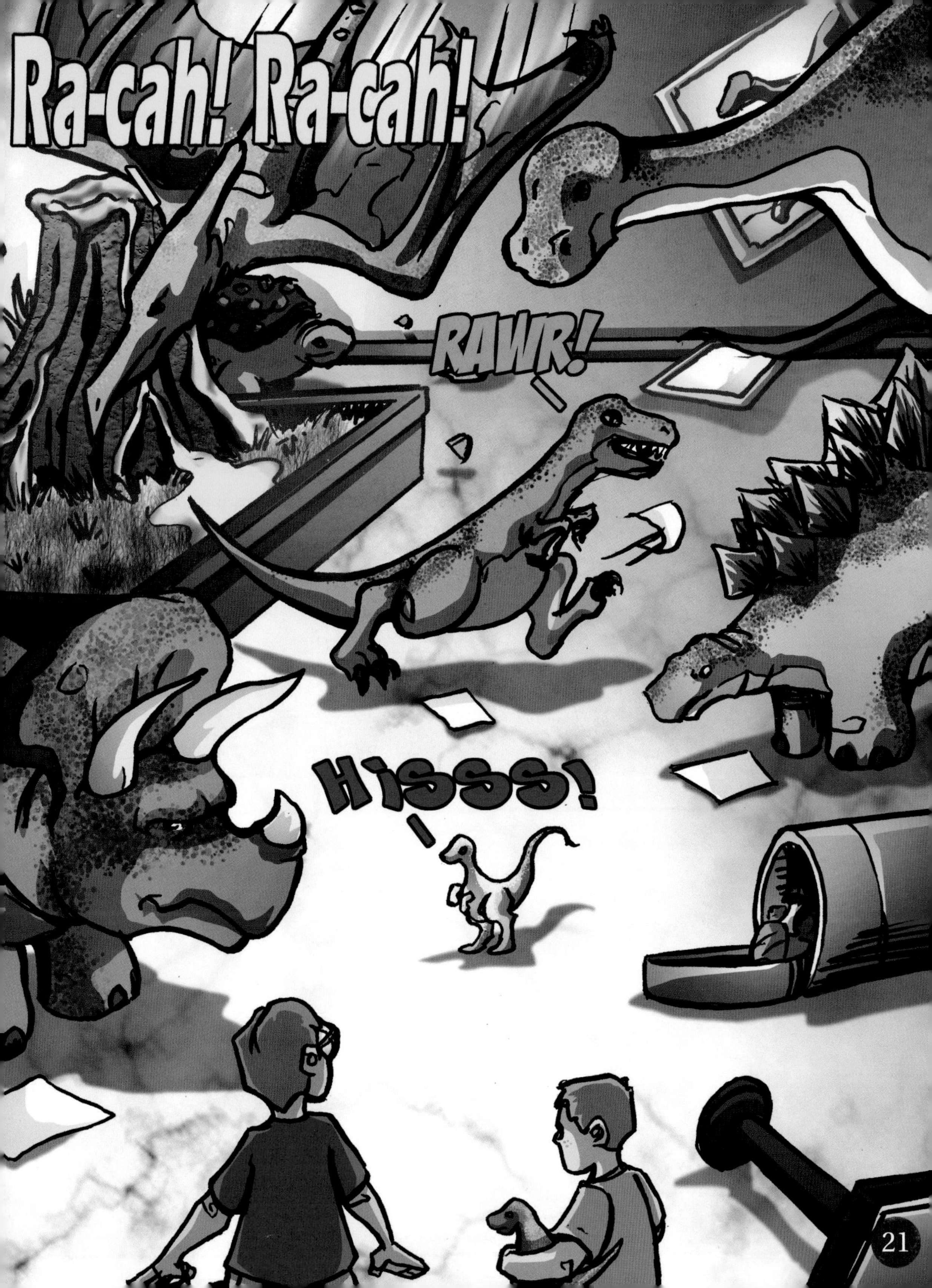
Ra-cah! Ra-cah!
RAWR!
HISSS!

MARVIN, CAN I USE YOUR TOY? I NEED IT TO DISTRACT THE DINOSAURS.

OKAY, COOL!

I'M GOING TO THROW THE TOY TO DISTRACT THE DINOSAURS. THEN I'M GOING TO MAKE A RUN FOR THE TRASH CAN TO GET THE PENCIL.

WHAT DO I DO?

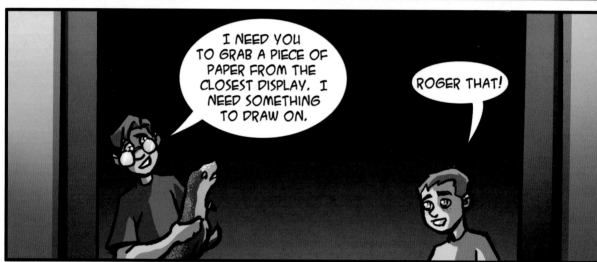

I NEED YOU TO GRAB A PIECE OF PAPER FROM THE CLOSEST DISPLAY. I NEED SOMETHING TO DRAW ON.

ROGER THAT!

HERE WE GO.

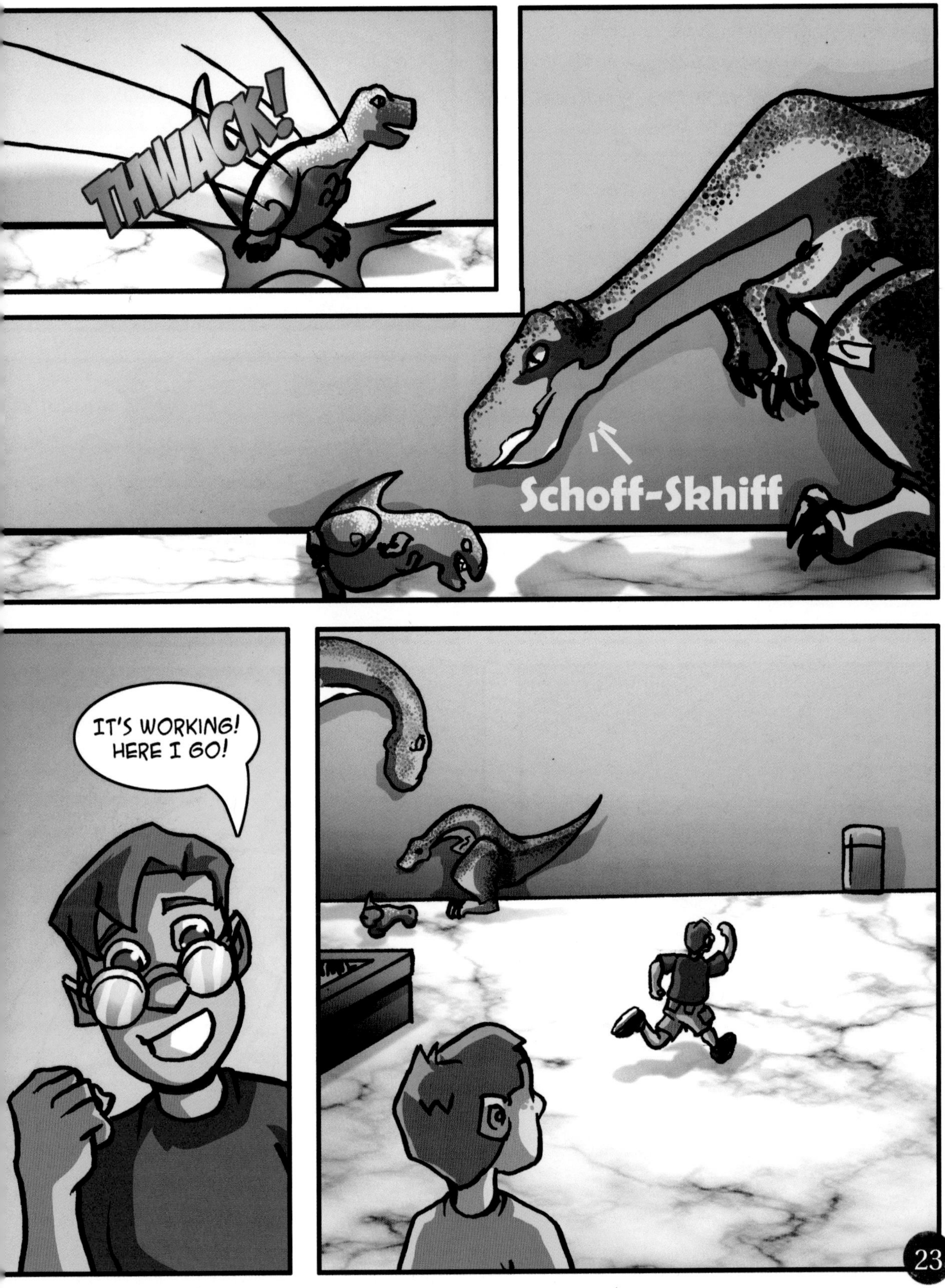
THWACK!
Schoff-Skhiff
IT'S WORKING! HERE I GO!

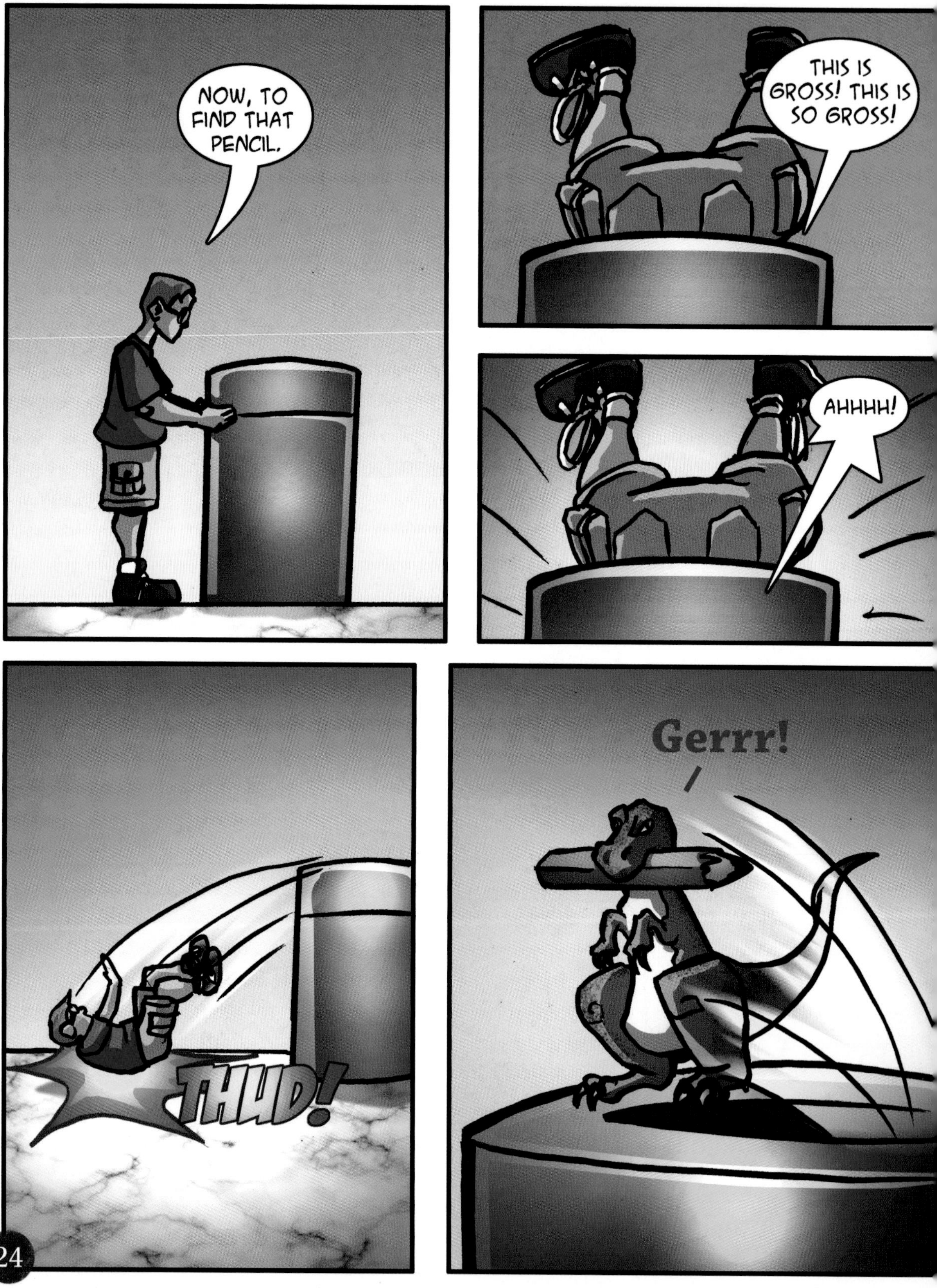
NOW, TO FIND THAT PENCIL.
THIS IS GROSS! THIS IS SO GROSS!
AHHHH!
THUD!
Gerrr!

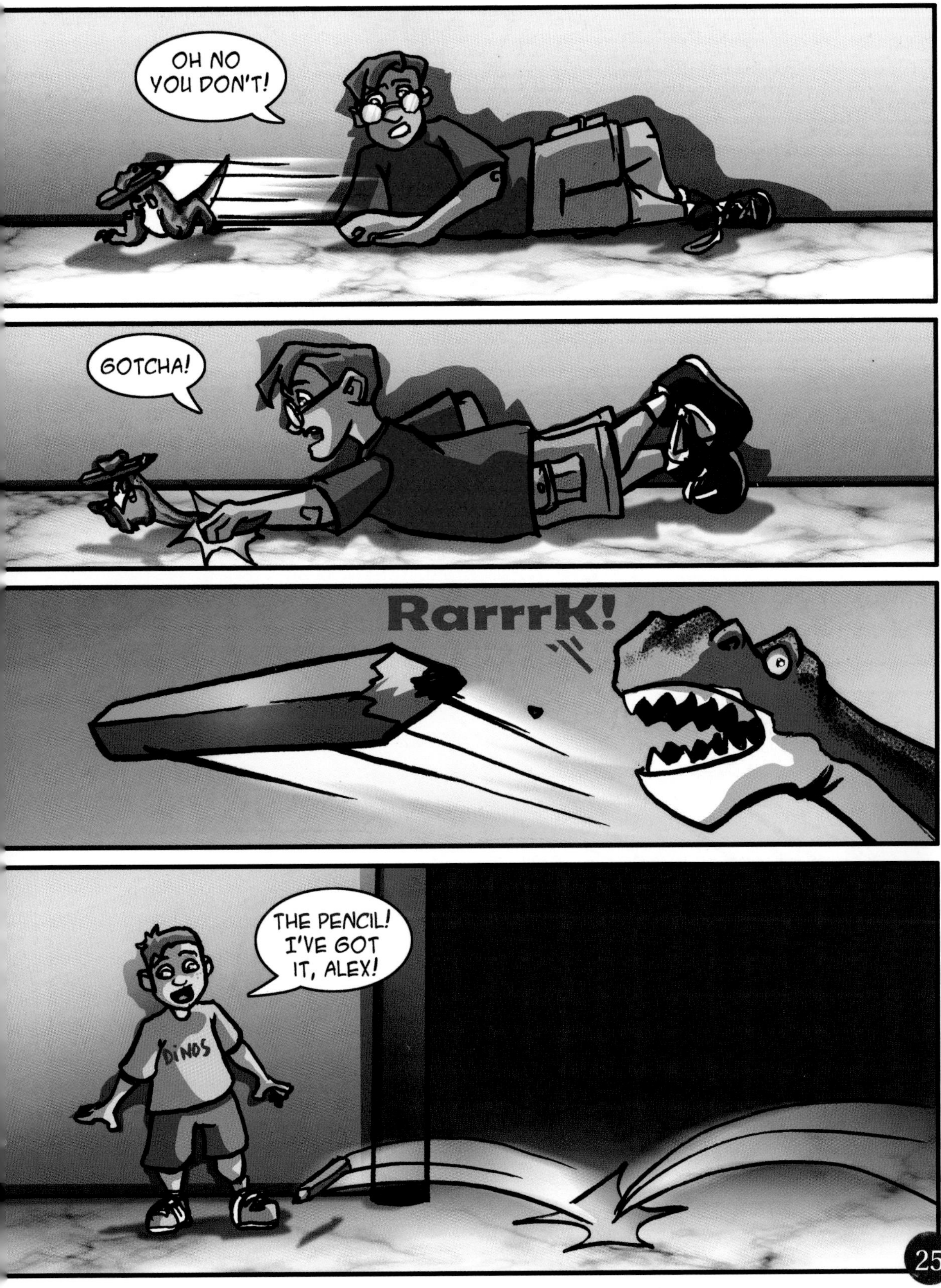
OH NO YOU DON'T!
GOTCHA!
RarrrK!
THE PENCIL! I'VE GOT IT, ALEX!

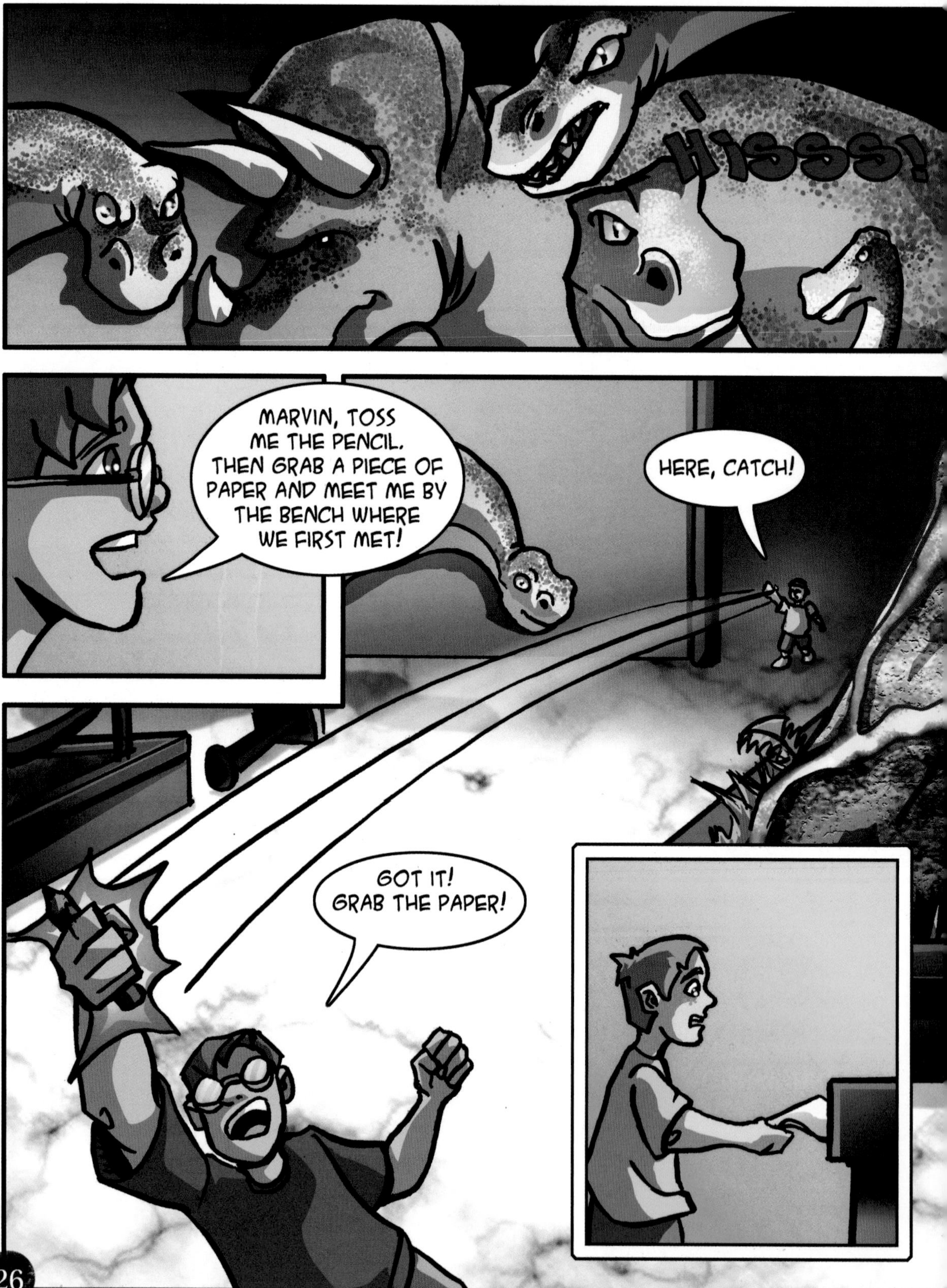
HISSSS!
MARVIN, TOSS ME THE PENCIL. THEN GRAB A PIECE OF PAPER AND MEET ME BY THE BENCH WHERE WE FIRST MET!
HERE, CATCH!
GOT IT! GRAB THE PAPER!

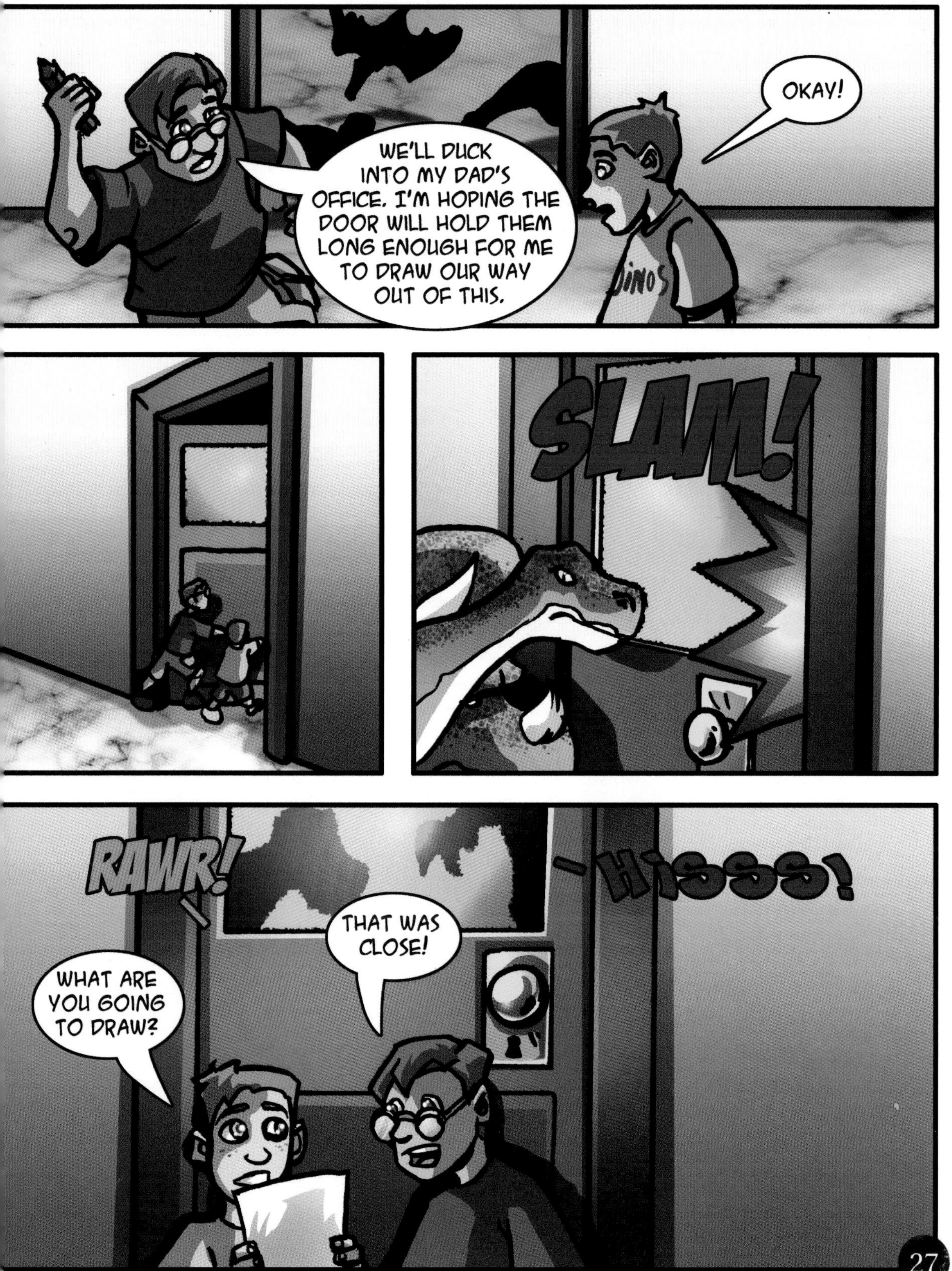
WE'LL DUCK INTO MY DAD'S OFFICE. I'M HOPING THE DOOR WILL HOLD THEM LONG ENOUGH FOR ME TO DRAW OUR WAY OUT OF THIS.
OKAY!
DINOS
SLAM!
RAWR!
HISSS!
THAT WAS CLOSE!
WHAT ARE YOU GOING TO DRAW?

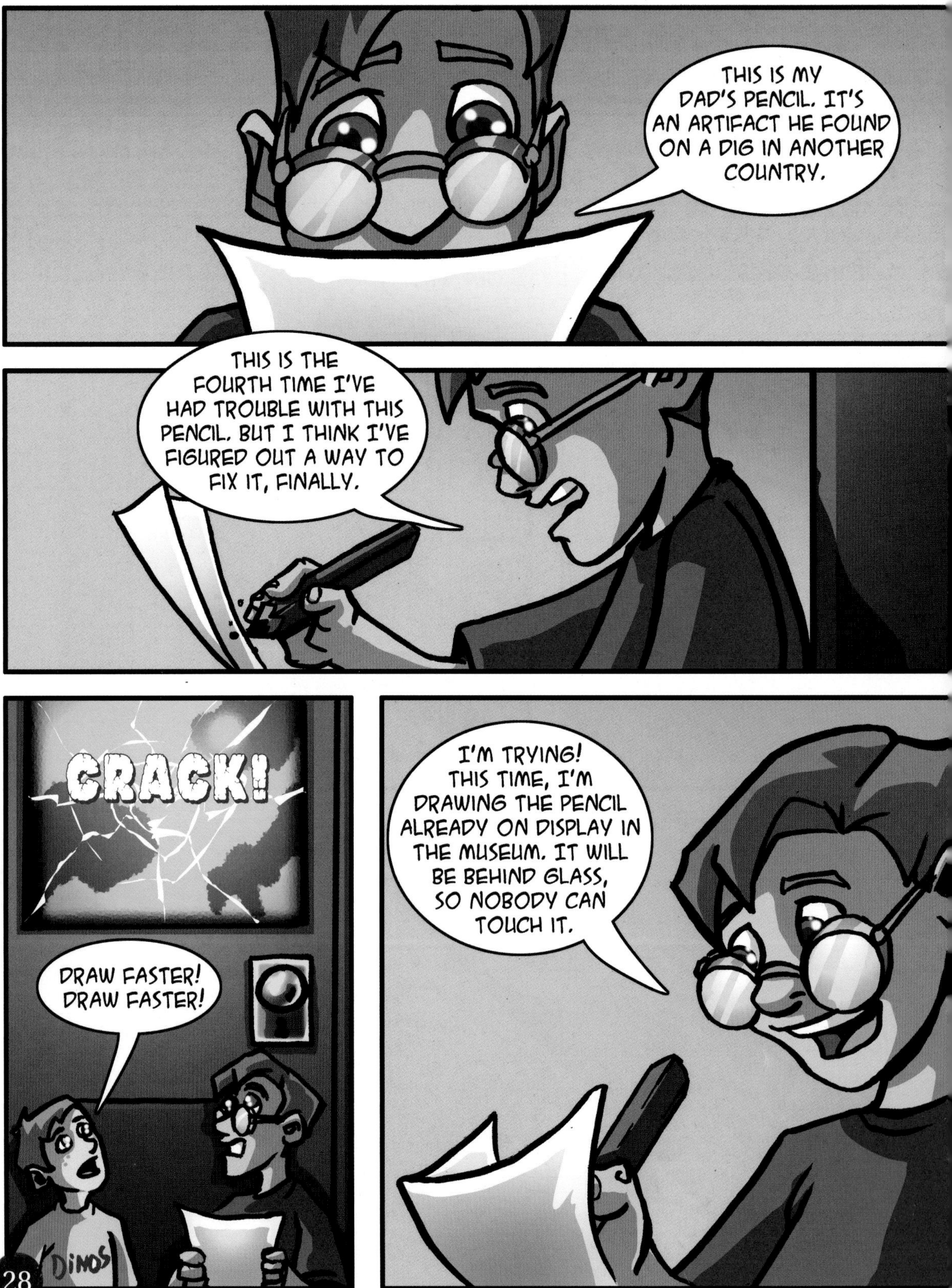
THIS IS MY DAD'S PENCIL. IT'S AN ARTIFACT HE FOUND ON A DIG IN ANOTHER COUNTRY.
THIS IS THE FOURTH TIME I'VE HAD TROUBLE WITH THIS PENCIL. BUT I THINK I'VE FIGURED OUT A WAY TO FIX IT, FINALLY.
CRACK!
DRAW FASTER! DRAW FASTER!
DINOS
I'M TRYING! THIS TIME, I'M DRAWING THE PENCIL ALREADY ON DISPLAY IN THE MUSEUM. IT WILL BE BEHIND GLASS, SO NOBODY CAN TOUCH IT.

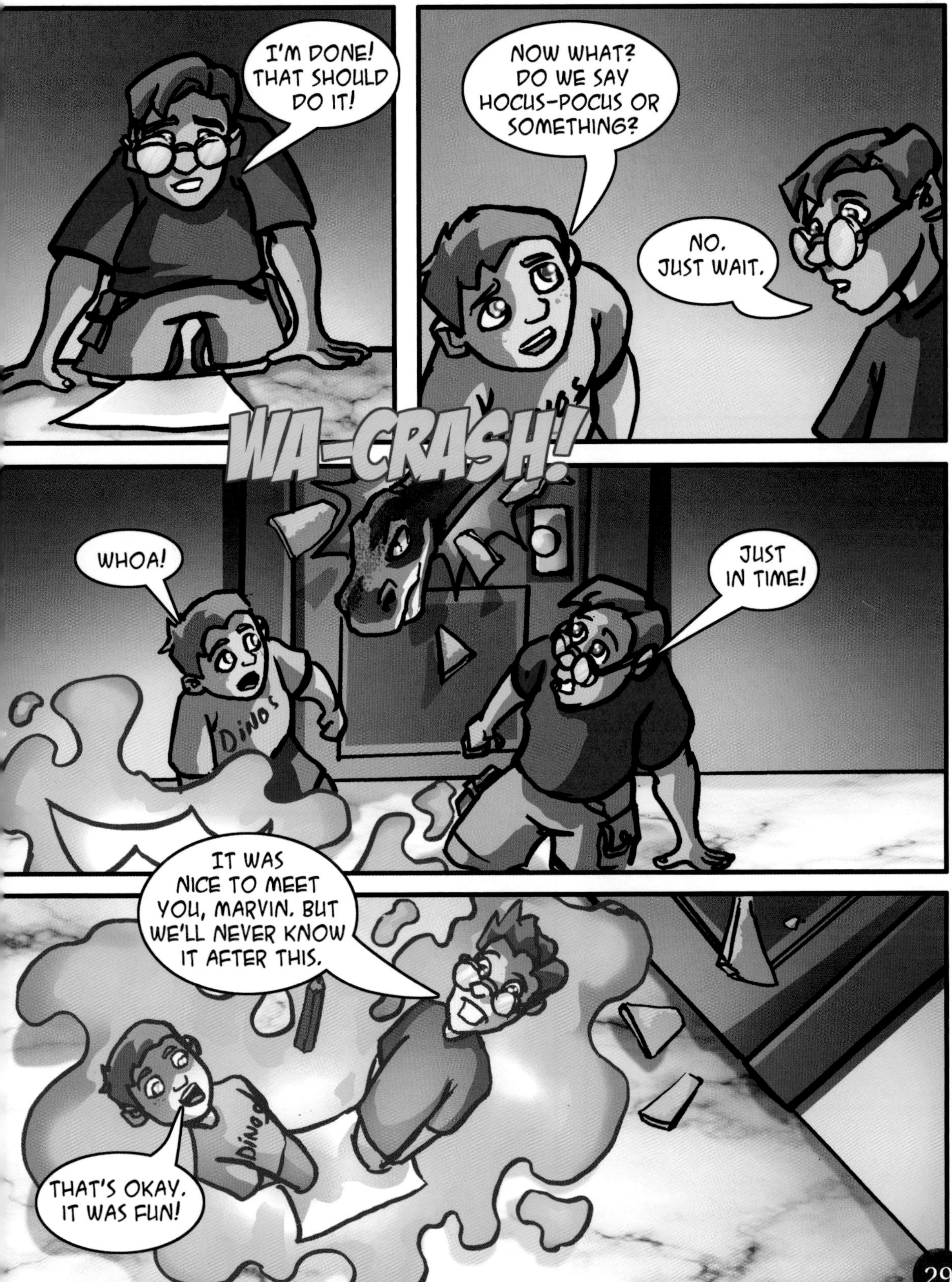
I'M DONE! THAT SHOULD DO IT!
NOW WHAT? DO WE SAY HOCUS-POCUS OR SOMETHING?
NO. JUST WAIT.
WA-CRASH!
WHOA!
JUST IN TIME!
IT WAS NICE TO MEET YOU, MARVIN. BUT WE'LL NEVER KNOW IT AFTER THIS.
THAT'S OKAY. IT WAS FUN!

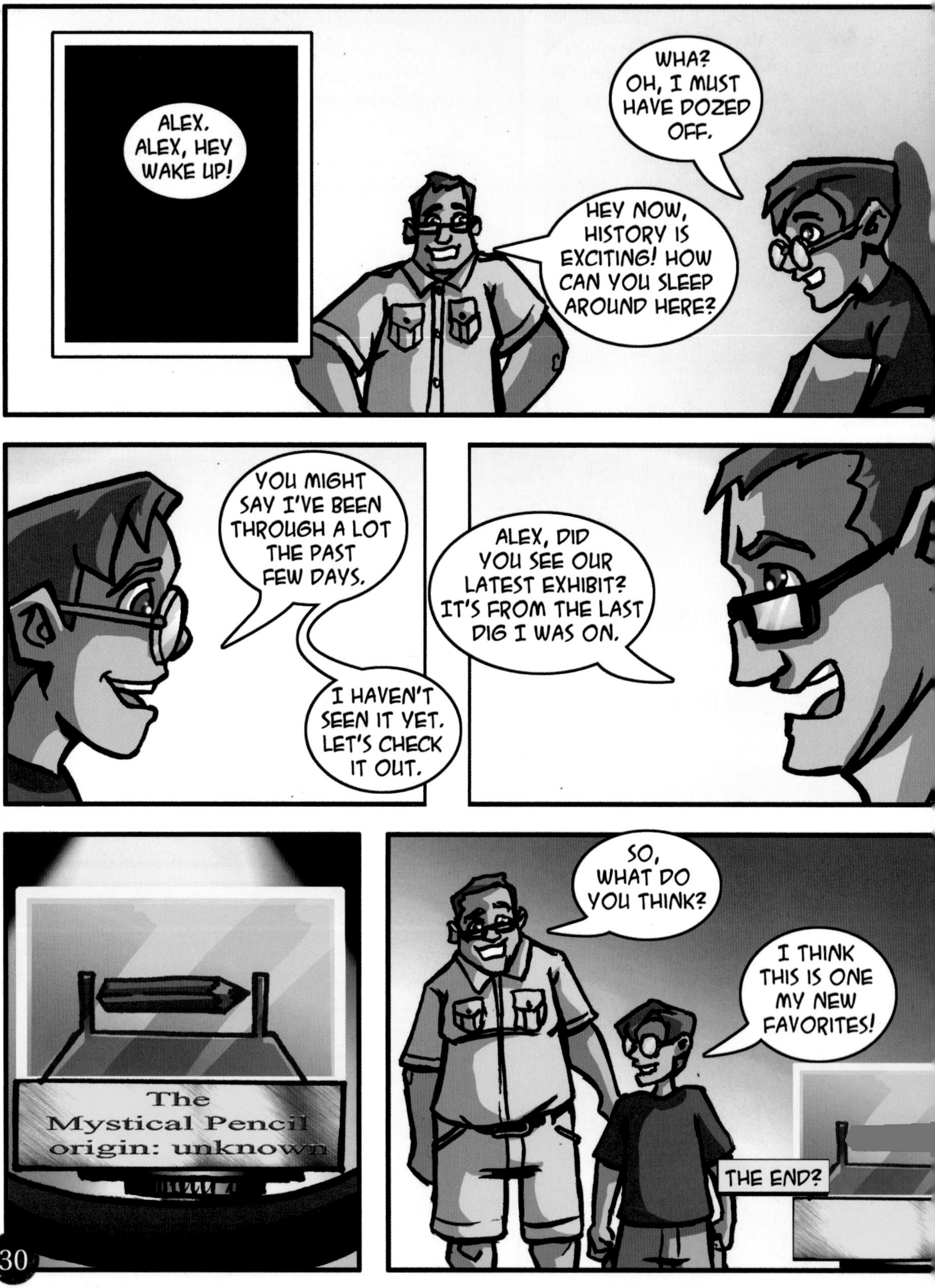
ALEX. ALEX, HEY WAKE UP!
WHA? OH, I MUST HAVE DOZED OFF.
HEY NOW, HISTORY IS EXCITING! HOW CAN YOU SLEEP AROUND HERE?
YOU MIGHT SAY I'VE BEEN THROUGH A LOT THE PAST FEW DAYS.
I HAVEN'T SEEN IT YET. LET'S CHECK IT OUT.
ALEX, DID YOU SEE OUR LATEST EXHIBIT? IT'S FROM THE LAST DIG I WAS ON.
The Mystical Pencil origin: unknown
SO, WHAT DO YOU THINK?
I THINK THIS IS ONE MY NEW FAVORITES!
THE END?

How to Draw a Dinosaur

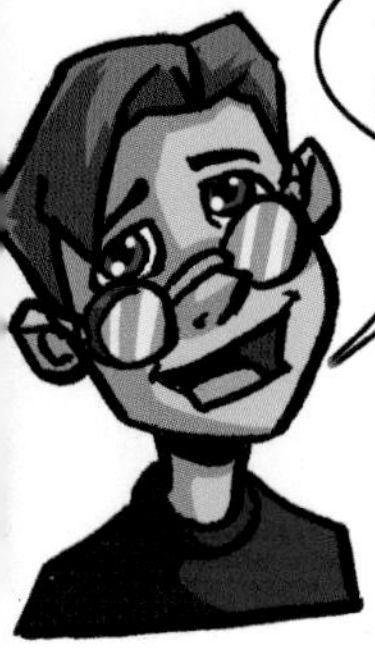

WE'RE GOING TO LEARN HOW TO DRAW A DINOSAUR!

YOU NEED A PENCIL, AN ERASER, AND SOME PAPER.

1

USE BASIC SHAPES TO SKETCH THE BODY. YOU CAN USE OVALS, CYLINDERS, AND A CONE FOR THE TAIL.

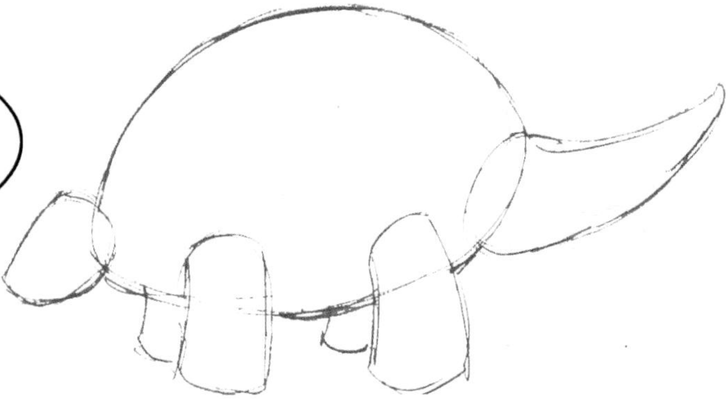

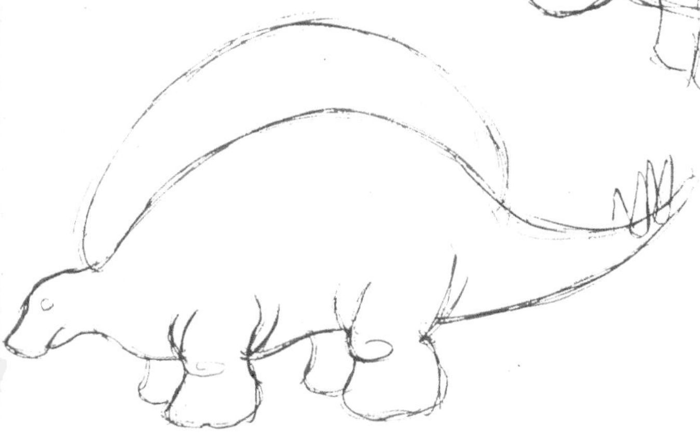

2

ERASE THE LINES YOU DON'T NEED, LIKE THE LINES BEHIND THE TAIL AND HEAD. ADD SOME DETAIL OUTLINES FOR THE SHAPE OF THE SPIKES, EYES, LEGS, AND FEET OF THE DINO.

3

FILL IN THE DETAILS FOR THE SPIKES, TOES, AND SKIN MARKINGS. HAVE FUN AND BE CREATIVE. YOU CAN RESEARCH OTHER IMAGES OF DINOSAURS IF YOU NEED HELP WITH IDEAS ON WHAT TO ADD TO YOUR DRAWING.

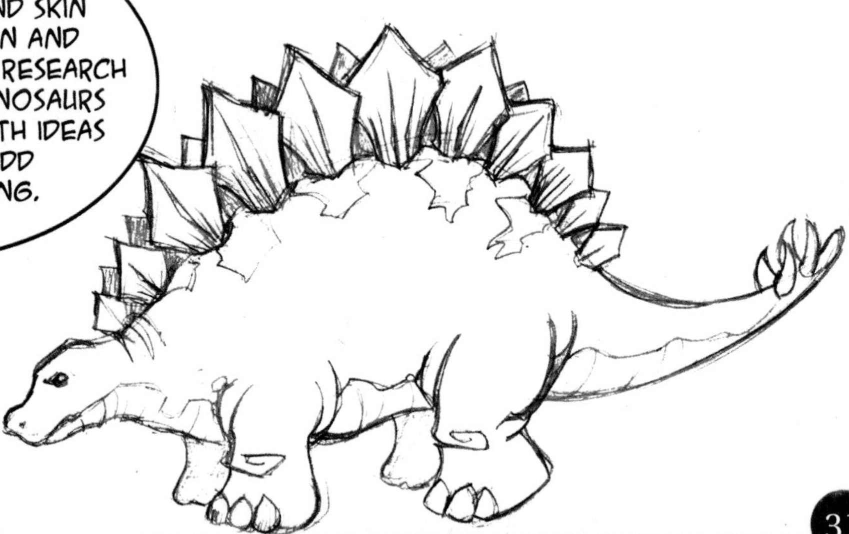

4

PRACTICE! AND HAVE FUN BRINGING YOUR ART TO LIFE!

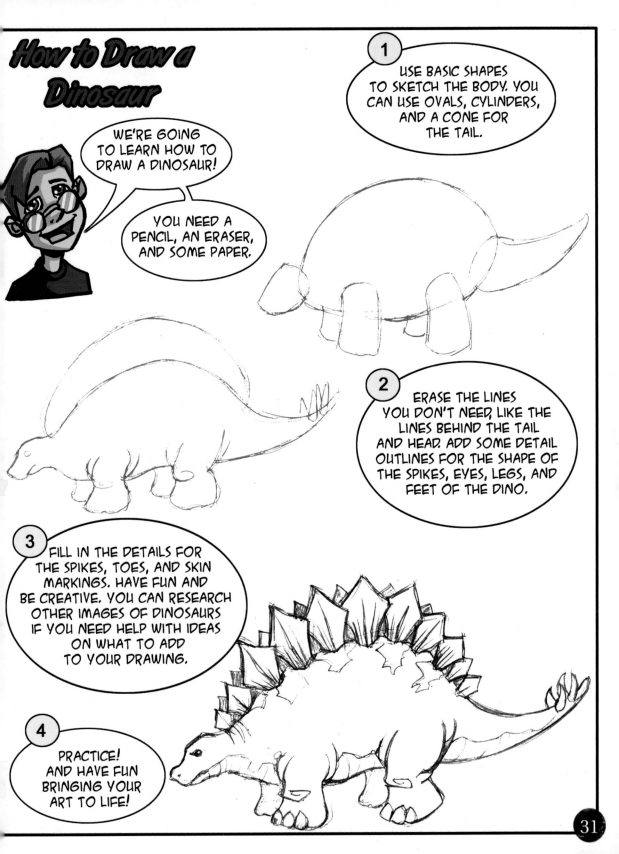

About the Author

Dustin Evans was born and raised in Oklahoma. In 2005, Dustin graduated from Oklahoma State University with a BFA in Graphic Design & Illustration. He has since gone on to work with such companies as Disney, IDW Publishing, Magic Wagon, and more. His work can be seen in comic books and children's books and on apparel and TV. He enjoys spending time with his family and pets, reading, drawing, and going to museums and movies.

Dustin begins each page with simple pencil and paper. Working from the script, he creates a rough layout for each page. Once the layouts are ready, he then scans the images into the computer to make them larger. The next step is to print out the larger layout, transfer it to the final page using a light box, and then ink the final image. Dustin then goes back to the computer to scan the final, inked image. Now it's time to add digital color, special effects, and lettering using computer programs. Finally, the image is complete and ready for print after some fine-tuning with any needed edits.

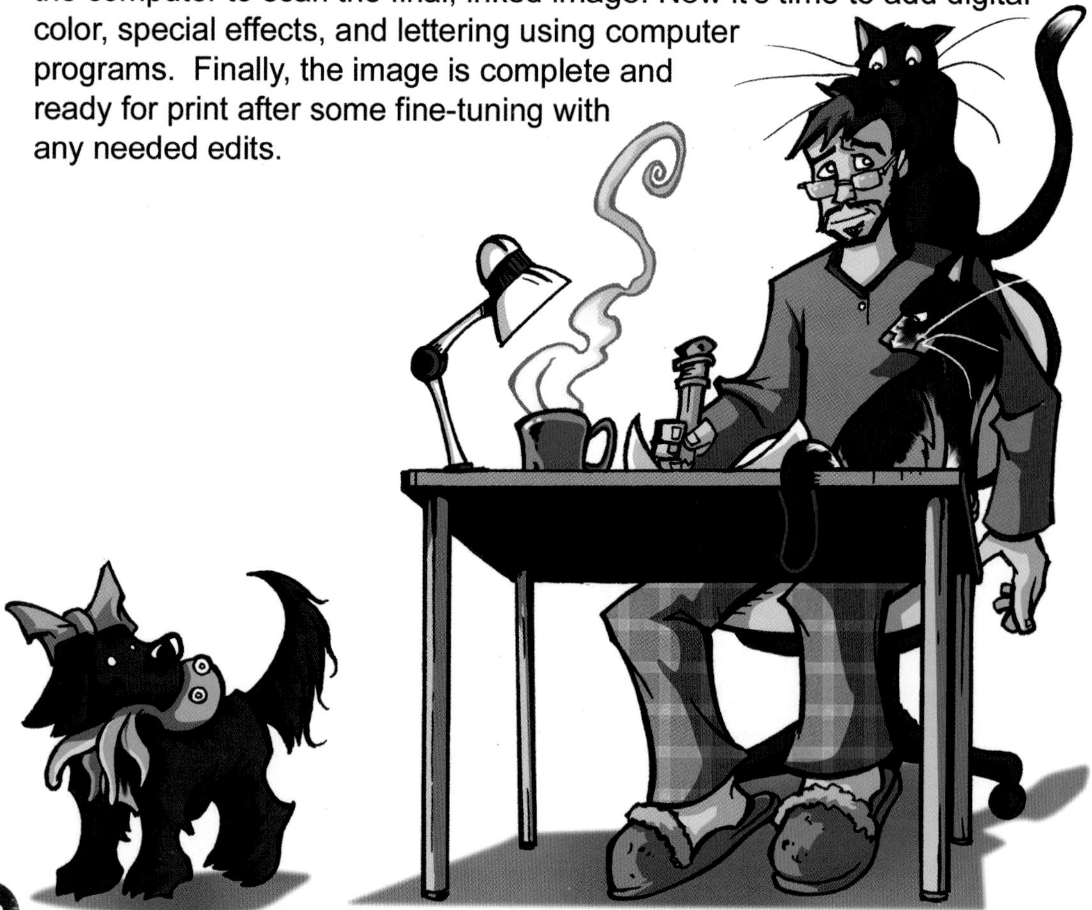